SECRET OF
THE SCARAB

Isabella Bassett

CONTENTS

Title Page

Copyright

Chapter 1   1

Chapter 2   9

Chapter 3   18

Chapter 4   27

Chapter 5   36

Chapter 6   45

Chapter 7   54

Chapter 8   63

Chapter 9   73

Chapter 10   82

Chapter 11   92

Chapter 12   102

Chapter 13   111

Chapter 14   121

Chapter 15   129

Chapter 16	138
Chapter 17	147
Chapter 18	158
Chapter 19	168
Chapter 20	179
Chapter 21	188
Chapter 22	198
Chapter 23	208
Chapter 24	218
Chapter 25	227
Chapter 26	236
Chapter 27	245
Chapter 28	252
Chapter 29	262
Chapter 30	271
Chapter 31	281
MORE BOOKS BY ISABELLA BASSETT	286

CHAPTER 1

Egypt, 1925

"Now, here is a civilization that knows what's important in this life," Uncle Albert said with some satisfaction as he looked up from the display case. "And the next," he opined as he returned his gaze to his query.

I received his statement with some reservation and struggled to keep my eyes from rolling discreetly.

"Beetles," he added by way of clarification, and tapped on the glass of the display case, in the event that I had any doubts as to his meaning. Having thus illuminated me, he went back to murmuring lovingly to the glass that separated him from the carved stone scarabs arranged behind it.

I cast a glance about the room—just one of the many at the Egyptian Museum in Cairo that still awaited our visit. The rest of the members of the Royal Society for Natural History Appreciation, of which my uncle was a constituent, were similarly preoccupied with various ancient Egyptian artifacts. From mummified cats and crocodiles, to plates painted with the heads of jackals, each aged member was bent over some dubious animal-themed treasure or other.

Though the museum itself was a grandiose affair, with airy atriums, columns and vaulted ceilings, meant to convey the majesty of the ancient Egyptian kingdoms it was employed to display, the room dedicated to its animal collection was small and faced externally. The Egyptian sun, even though it was November and early in the morning, was unrelenting. It streamed in through the tall windows, bounced off the glass cases with blinding clarity, and lit up the sand particles dancing lethargically in the air.

The folded newspaper I fanned in front of my face did little to shift the thick layers of air, which felt as though they had not moved from this room since the last mummy had breathed out. Or perhaps it only seemed that way because my uncle and I had been staring at the same scarabs for the past twenty minutes.

Someone had opened a window—rather optimistically—but the aperture was proving to be quite impotent at freshening up the room.

"Fascinating creatures, beetles," my uncle continued. "The Creator himself must have been fond of a good coleopteran, as he fashioned so many of them."

"Ah, very well observed," the eager young man, named Reginald or Tobias, I could not recall, a visiting fellow from the British Museum, who had been assigned to guide us through the museum, said as he sidled up to my uncle's side. "Why, there are over 30,000 species of dung beetle alone. Boggles the mind," he concluded.

Ah, dung beetles! Reginald, or Tobias, had hit upon the very reason we were in Egypt.

"And it doesn't stop with beetles," Uncle Albert said, warming up to his favorite topic. "The divinity of insects was well understood by ancient civilizations. The ancient Athenians wore golden grasshopper pins on their togas to show that they were of pure Athenian lineage. And the Swedes believed that the devil used dragonflies to weigh people's souls."

"Which, in a strange and interesting way, relates to the stone scarabs, fashioned after the dung beetle, you see here," the young scholar said, jumping in to test his entomological prowess against my uncle. "The ancient Egyptians believed that the god Anubis weighed the purity of one's heart against a feather before one was admitted to pass through the underworld into paradise. As the heart was suspected to be too truthful and could get its owner into trouble, these stone scarabs were used to replace the heart and ensure an unfettered passage into the afterlife. Beetles were placed in tombs to guarantee the immortality of the soul.

The dung beetle, in particular, was associated with rebirth..."

The rest of the discussion between the young man and my uncle about the intricacies of beetles, and their rightful place in the pantheon of gods, was lost to a droning buzz in my head that sounded very much like the flight of a May beetle.

I caught James' eye across the room and smiled. He was similarly attached to Lord Packenham, who was peering inside the contents of another display case further down the gallery. James smiled back and pushed a wayward lock of sandy hair from his brow. I let my gaze linger on his handsome features for a few moments.

While James and I had recently come to an understanding, we were in Egypt in our professional capacities—he, as Lord Packenham's private secretary, and I, as my uncle's. And as Lord Packenham and my uncle were the most bitter of rivals when it came to beetle collecting, or any other business to do with the Royal Society, James and I had to keep a professional distance and to ensure that our respective employers emerged victorious in the latest competition.

Much like the artifacts in the museum, the Royal Society itself was a collection of ancient specimens of the British peerage, some as ancient as the mummies on display. The Society was a place to which peers of the realm were deposited after retirement, by exasperated wives and loving families, for safe-keeping. As the name suggested, the Society's chief concern was the study of natural history. To that end, they traveled to exotic places, such as France, Italy or Switzerland, and terrorized the natives with their harebrained contest over insects or flowers.

My gaze lingered on the Society's fellows shuffling about the room on stiff legs, hunchbacked, from one display case to another. Clearly, the room held many delights for the aged members, while their private secretaries, like me, or James, or awkward Alistair, or vile Hector, stood around with vacant stares.

It was not that I did not appreciate the wonders Egypt had to offer. In fact, I was quite looking forward to our trip up the Nile and visiting all the ancient temples and monuments one had only seen in picture books. But one was allowed to feel fairly sulky when a promised trip to the Pyramids of Giza and the Sphinx was so cruelly postponed in favor of an extended examination of the entirety of the museum's collection of mummified animals in storage.

"A beetle god, a jackal god, a god with the face of a baboon," my uncle was saying, "yes, one can tell by their appreciation of nature that the ancient Egyptians were quite advanced in their understanding of the natural order of things. Fascinating."

While the atmosphere in the gallery this

morning was one of quiet respectability and scholarly contemplation, it belied the true purpose of the Royal Society's presence in Egypt. This was the calm before the storm, as they say. The members of the Society were just lolling away the days before they could embark upon a cut-throat tournament of beetle collecting.

At stake, this time, was a mummified cat belonging to Lord Lackbryne, who had recently inherited it from a deceased relation. However, as Lady Lackbryne refused to have any such creature in the house, it was judged by the Royal Society that the article should be entered into general circulation as one of the coveted annual prizes of the Society.

The need for a new prize was due to the dissolution of the Golden Platypus—a name that was at odds with the specimen's moth-eaten state. The stuffed animal, which for years had been the top annual prize of the Society, had sadly met its end in the vaults of the Bank of England, eaten by the Bank's resident rats. But as the Society blamed Uncle Albert for the animal's demise—he had placed the Golden Platypus in the vault for safeguarding—the less said about the matter, the better.

I approved of the new prize wholeheartedly because, as an attempt at poetical symmetry, the Society had decided that a visit to Egypt was warranted for the inaugural use of the mummified trophy. A plan was devised for the members, and their retinue, to spend a leisurely jaunt up the River Nile, punctuating visits to ancient ruins with excursions for beetle collecting. The member who collected the most beetles would win the prize. Furthermore, as this was Egypt, extra points would be awarded to the member who amassed the most stone scarabs. To that end, requests were sent to various archeological digs in the Valley of the Kings, but an invitation had yet to materialize.

Though the members of the Royal Society lingered cheerfully in the gallery, there was tension in the air. The museum's director, a Frenchman, was huffing in a corner. His indignation stemmed from having been strong-armed by the British High Commissioner to close down the museum this morning for the exclusive use of the Royal Society. This put the director in a difficult position—tourists were clamoring to come into the museum, and a near riot was breaking out by the front doors, but the British High Commissioner was not a man to be trifled with.

The delay, however, was giving the local salesmen ample time to ply their beads and imitation scarabs on the hapless bystanders, as witnessed through the open window.

A local man stood quietly by the director's side, observing our group. The young man was dressed in a European suit, but wore a fez, a combination that I'd been told was favored by the educated strata of Egyptian society. The fez had instantaneously ingratiated him to my uncle, who was a fez connoisseur in his own right. Since arriving in Egypt, emboldened by the ubiquitous use of the red topper here, my uncle had taken to wearing his own specimen outside the confines of his private rooms. In fact, we were scheduled to pay a visit to my uncle's local maker in the market the following day.

Moving to the opposite side of the scarab case, Uncle Albert adjusted the fez perched atop his fluffy white hair, though it threatened to slip off again once he looked down at the display case.

But there was something else that the young Egyptian man wore that had attracted my uncle's attention even more. He displayed the most singular scarab shaped pin on his lapel. Uncle Albert's covert glances towards it gave me to understand that he quite admired it. Between peeks, my uncle stroked his own lapel, no doubt wishing he had such an adornment. I had it in mind to ask the young man where one could procure such a skewer for my uncle, when the doors to the room crashed open, and a harried man of a bedraggled appearance entered.

CHAPTER 2

The new arrival nodded towards the director, but did not approach to greet him. The director stared at the untidy man with contempt.

I observed the newcomer with some interest. In his mid-thirties, thus about a decade older than me, the man's floppy hair and nonchalant outfit singled him out as an Englishman. His deep tan, layer of fine sand on his clothes, and some sort of Egyptian amulet—an eagle with spread wings—suspended from his neck on a thin leather strap, further identified him as either a desert adventurer or an archaeologist. There were many of those hanging about the bar at the Shepheard's Hotel, hunting for willing listeners to their tales of glory and exploits.

"I say," said the man to no one in particular and approached Uncle Albert as he was closest to the door. "Are you the members of the Royal Society for Natural History Appreciation?"

Uncle Albert straightened up and puffed out his chest at the compliment of being recognized as a member of such a distinguished institution.

"Terribly sorry, and all that," the newcomer continued without waiting for a reply. "Delay at the Department of Antiquities."

My uncle mirrored some of the museum director's countenance and stared at the newcomer with an expression of utter confusion.

"Forgive me, how silly of me. I'm Nigel, Nigel Hargrave," the man continued in a breathless manner. "The younger son of Lord Chatfield, though my brother, of course, bears the title now. Business with the Antiquities office brought my brother and me to Cairo unexpectedly. And I rushed here as soon as I heard the Royal Society was in Egypt."

And after further nudging of the brain and a lot of eyebrow-lifting, Uncle Albert seemed to get the train on the right track because he exclaimed, "Nigel, my boy! Good to see you!" They shook hands. "I'm Albert. Haven't seen you since you were in short trousers. Terribly sorry about that uncle of yours, by the way," my uncle said and gestured to the newspaper in my hand. On the front page of the newspaper I was holding was a sensational article about the latest Egyptian curse that had caused the death of someone in England. Presumably it was Mr. Hargrave's uncle.

I gazed upon the dust-covered man with newfound curiosity.

"Yes, though he was a rather estranged from us," Mr. Hargrave said, waving off the condolences.

"One wishes, though, that the newspapers would not make such a fuss, talking about a curse and all that rot. I would rather they focused on the historical importance of our find. But all the public cares about is that silly curse."

By now, the rest of the Society's members had gathered round, and a ripple of joy passed through the collective body as they learned who the Englishman was.

"Archibald's son," my uncle said to the members who were still in the dark.

They nodded appreciatively.

"Poor old Baldo, such a gifted chap," my uncle continued. "Too bad they could not cut off the leg on time to stop the poison from spreading. Just as well."

"My father died of a snake bite," Mr. Hargrave said, turning to me. "An Indian saw-scaled viper, *Echis carinatus*." My uncle nodded appreciatively at the binomial nomenclature, and I gave a silent thanks that my uncle was not given to quite such dangerous adventures. "Father kept a terrarium of sorts in his greenhouse at Swellington Hall, near Lower Swell, not far from Stow-on-the-Wold, if you know it, where he retired to after he returned from Egypt," Mr. Hargrave continued. "No one quite understands how he found himself inside the enclosure, where he was discovered the next morning. Somehow, he had fallen through the glass roof. It could not have helped that he was wearing a decidedly green jacket, which made him look like a lizard. But he insisted it helped him blend in with the environment and appear more congenial to the snakes. Of course, the whole family was at Barton in the Beans at the time, not far from Sheepy Magna, and with the servants refusing to set foot near the greenhouse, on account of all my father's hobbies, no one was there to come to his aid."

"A brilliant mind," my uncle said with admiration.

Mr. Hargrave nodded. Though I, for my share, wondered at the man's wisdom of dressing like a lizard around snakes, especially given the way he'd met his end.

"Although I cannot help but think that he would not have been struck down so early and so suddenly if he had not always been pottering about with insects and things. Tarantula hawk wasps, bald-faced hornets, bullet ants..." Mr. Hargrave said.

This veiled jab at the core recreation of the Royal Society, however, seemed to be lost on my uncle.

"Ah," my uncle began, dreamily, "to die among the things one loves. That is the hope of every member of the Royal Society, I should think. I'm sure old Baldo died a happy man."

Mr. Hargrave nodded with hesitation.

"Baldo was always the adventurous one of

the Society," Uncle Albert continued reminiscing. "Never really made it to a meeting, always off to somewhere exotic. But it was an honor to have him as a member of the Society, of course," he concluded with a touch of commendation in his voice. "And I see that you and your brother followed in his footsteps. The article in the newspaper related your brother's success at finding some unexpected...find." My uncle was lost for words where beetles and insects were not concerned. He tried a second time: "An important find of some sorts..." Then, giving up, pointed helplessly towards the newspaper in my hands.

A shadow passed over Mr. Hargrave's face.

"My brother Eustace may have the money and may provide the financial backing for our dig at Luxor, but his understanding of ancient Egyptian history is basic at best. However my brother means to misrepresent his role in this discovery to the newspapers, the fact remains that I am the lead archaeologist of the dig. Why, Eustace can't tell a canopic jar from a cartonnage," the young man said and chuckled with contempt at his brother's shortcomings.

It seemed my uncle had inadvertently stumbled upon a point of contention between the two brothers, and he communicated his confusion as to how to proceed by going red and blinking rapidly.

After a moment, Mr. Hargrave realized his

own blunder of becoming vexed by my uncle's comment and cleared his throat. "But let's not argue over such trifles. My father always spoke very fondly of the Society." My uncle beamed back at him, the misunderstanding forgotten. "And I came to the museum this morning because while at the Department of Antiquities, I heard that the Royal Society was looking for an archeological dig to visit."

"By Jove, yes!" came the unanimous cries of the Lords who, until this moment, had simply been observing the proceedings and nodding silently at salient points in the narrative surrounding the former member's untimely death.

"Well, I would like to extend an invitation to the Society to visit our dig at Luxor," Mr. Hargrave said with great enthusiasm. I wondered if he realized what he was getting himself into. But perhaps, having grown up with a Royal Society member as a father, he was well versed in the Society's follies.

"Luxor?" rose Lord Fetherly's voice. "Are we going there?"

A confused murmur passed through the crowd.

"I am sure you are going to stop off at Luxor," Mr. Hargrave said. "Everybody does."

"We are," James confirmed.

"What's that?" asked Lord Mantelbury, who was even harder of hearing than the rest of the members.

"He's invited us to his archeological site," Lord Packenham said in a raised voice. "You know, the one in the newspapers," he added, as though he was speaking to a child.

"Oh, jolly good," said Lord Mantelbury. I was not certain he'd quite grasped Lord Packenham's meaning.

"The one with the curse?" Lord Fetherly inquired more astutely.

Mr. Hargrave nodded. "Just the one," he said with an edge to his voice.

"Oh, jolly good—"

"Capital—"

"That's just the ticket—" cried the chorus of Lords.

"Any good beetle hunting round there?" said Lord Mantelbury, going for the jugular.

Mr. Hargrave looked slightly perplexed by the question, but recovered quickly. "You mean scarabs? Yes, plenty of those to be found." He smiled at the Lords gathered around him, but some of the earlier enthusiasm seemed to have flickered out of his face.

While the archeologist was undoubtedly referring to carved stone scarabs, I was certain that the members of the Society were mostly after the living things. I was left with the impression that this would be the first of many misunderstandings between Mr. Hargrave and the Royal Society.

"What an unlucky chap," Uncle Albert was saying as we were making our way out of the museum at last.

"You mean Mr. Hargrave?"

He nodded. "To have opened the only cursed tomb in Egypt," my uncle said.

I started to correct him and to point out that the 5th Earl of Carnarvon had died not three years ago, allegedly due to the curse of Tutankhamen. But I didn't want to confuse matters.

"You don't really believe in such things?" I asked cautiously.

"One has to look at these things critically," Uncle Albert said sagely. "Look at the facts. First his father, old Baldo, then his uncle. Mr. Hargrave is one unlucky young man."

"How long ago did Mr. Hargrave's father die?"

"Oh, more than ten years now."

"So his death can't really be related to the tomb Mr. Hargrave and his brother are currently excavating."

"Ah, these things work in mysterious ways," Uncle Albert said and tapped the side of his nose. "All I can tell you is, I'm glad young Alistair has booked us a private boat up the Nile. I would rather not spend too much time near Mr. Hargrave. Some of his bad luck might rub off on us."

I laughed, and exited the museum, plunging into the mid-day heat of Cairo with my arm through Uncle Albert's elbow.

Despite my uncle's misgivings, I was quite looking forward to meeting Mr. Hargrave again in Luxor. Nothing was more rousing to the spirit than a good Egyptian curse.

CHAPTER 3

As was well known among the members of our family, and our loyal servants, Uncle Albert's infamous fez came from a maker in Cairo. The days before the arrival of a new topper were always garnished with nervous energy. Evenings were spent before the mirror, pondering whether the new fez would be as good as its predecessors, and whether it would sit on top of the down-like hair just right. On the day of the fez's arrival, Uncle Albert tended to be uncharacteristically irascible, and the servants had learned to keep to their quarters until they heard their employer cavorting through the corridors, wearing his new hat.

Invariably, the fez that arrived was of impeccable craftsmanship and quality, and all my uncle's worries had been for nought.

It was thus decided that upon arrival in Cairo, my uncle would visit this conjurer of felt and steam, Mr. El Tarabishi, at his workshop. The event was preceded by months of fervent correspondence between uncle and fez maker, and today's date was settled upon as the day of the monumental meeting.

The fez workshop was located somewhere deep in the Cairo Market. Having refused any help from local guides, *dragomans*, and priding himself on his navigation skills, Uncle Albert set off for the shop using only a crudely drawn diagram acquired from the hotel's concierge.

The concierge had questioned the wisdom of my uncle's choice to find the shop on his own, but meeting with Uncle Albert's impenetrable stubbornness, had explained that locating the shop should not give my uncle too much trouble and supplied him with a hand-drawn map. The shop was located on the street of the Tent-makers, Hat-makers, Cloth-weavers, and Tailors, which I thought was quite a neat arrangement.

Though he declined a dragoman, Uncle Albert did not refuse my company, and we set off for the market together. Cairo was a bustling city, and I looked forward to a noisy and colorful market.

I mused at how our roles had reversed. While my mother had shipped me off to be Uncle Albert's secretary so he could look after me, and to prevent me from getting into any more trouble in London, I now felt responsible for Uncle, and worried that he might get himself into an unpleasant predicament. And with Uncle Albert, that was always a very possible risk.

Our driver deposited us at one end of the market, as his cab could go no further. He gave us a curious look and said something under his breath, shaking his head.

But my uncle was nothing if not a hardened subject of the British Empire, and, like many of his generation, possessed something of the Cecil Rhodes spirit. So he smiled in a self-satisfied manner, professed that he could read a map as well as any man, and dove into the activity of the market.

Within moments, we had lost our way and were stuck somewhere between the spices and the carpets, with no idea which way to turn.

The Cairo market was like nothing I had experienced before. The alleyways were teaming with people. Crowds were so thick, we could hardly make our way between the bodies. The contents of the stores seemed to all hang outside, and people shouted from all sides. It was hard to tell who was selling, who was buying, and who was simply giving vociferous advice.

The experience was quite disorienting. But by about the third time round the market, it became clear that each trade seemed to have its own quarter, with all shops of the same type clustered together: the metalworkers, the spice sellers, the shoemakers. Trouble was, we could not find the street with the fez-makers.

In each quarter, we played a game of charades, pointing to Uncle Albert's fez and asking for the way to Mr. El Tarabishi's shop. And in each quarter, we were given clear hand signals on how to get there. But somehow, we always ended up in a different quarter than the one we were meant to find. By the time the coppersmiths had sent us to the ironmongers, who forwarded us on to the furniture makers, who then showed us the way to the sweetmeat vendors, I was beginning to suspect that we were sent to the wrong quarters on purpose.

Trouble was that the game of charades was getting harder to play. Our hands were progressively filled with purchases—a pound of cumin, a small prayer carpet, and a much larger rug, just about the right size for a ballroom, which was to be delivered to the hotel by that afternoon, a pair of intricately detailed metal lamps, a tooled-leather folding stool, and a pair of embroidered slippers, in the Egyptian fashion, to go with Uncle's fez.

We hit upon the lane of cloth sellers and all related trades, quite unexpectedly, and were surprised by the transformation of the market at this end. Turning a corner, the correct lane opened up in front of us like a peaceful oasis. As we entered, all the noises of the market melted away —gone were the cries of the fruit sellers and the water-carriers—and we walked into a much more subdued affair.

My ears rang with the abrupt quietude. At first, I wondered if the calmness was due to the dampening effect of the cloth hanging all around us, absorbing all the noise. But then I noticed that the street seemed quite deserted. The stores were open, and all the clothes for sale hung outside, but the shopkeepers were not before their stores.

We proceeded down the narrow lane, gazing at the indecipherable—to us—signs, looking for clues as to the fez shop, but we were not having much luck.

Down the lane, a small group of men had gathered before a shop front, sitting around in the manner I had seen local men take tea, and we hastened to ask them for directions. I mentally prepared that my uncle was about to walk away with a jalabiya tunic, accessorized by a kaftan, and finished off with enough cloth for a turban. At least they would pair well with his new slippers and fez, if we ever discovered the shop, anyway.

As the men saw us approach, a general cry emitted from their midst, whether of joy was difficult to tell. A few of the more sprightly ones got up and dashed our way, arms outstretched to heaven, shouting something at us. It was quite the reception, if that's what it was.

All of them wore the traditional long tunics favored by Egyptian men. But as they walked towards us, another man, one dressed in a European suit and a fez, much like the man at the museum, pushed his way through.

"Welcome. We have been expecting you," he said to us in accented English as he approached us.

"But I am sorry that you have come all this way. You cannot visit the fez shop today."

"What?!" I exclaimed in return. Was this the fez maker? He was no older than me, and younger than I expected the fez-maker to be. Why was he turning us away? Had the other shop owners objected to our visit? Is that why they were gathered in front of his store?

"Look here," Uncle Albert began, "you can't push us away. We've been all over this infernal market. This seems like the right place! I can see the shop sign, right there." Uncle Albert pointed to a sign, reminiscent of a scarab, above the store in front of which the men had been sitting. "It's the same as the maker stamp in my fez," he protested.

I could tell Uncle Albert was getting quite worked up about it. He was seething with indignation at having come this close to his favorite fez maker only to be turned away. I could see why the servants kept their distance from him on fez-day.

The young man didn't budge. Neither did the men behind him, who stood shoulder to shoulder, barring our way.

"We are here to see Mr. El Tarabishi, the fez maker," I said, trying to keep my voice level. We would gain nothing by being rude to these men.

"I know. I understand. But today is impossible," the young man insisted. "Please, go back to your hotel."

It was then that I noticed that he was wearing the same scarab pin as the man in the museum. Frowning, I looked at him more closely. Could this be the same man? But no, he was not. What was the meaning of all this?

"I have an invitation," Uncle Albert said, having pulled a letter from Mr. El Tarabishi out of his pocket.

"I know, Lord Tatham. It was I who has been writing to you," the young man said.

The statement caught me by surprise. Had we been lured into a trap?

"You? You are Mr. El Tarabishi?" my uncle asked. I could hear the wariness in his voice. We had both expected someone different.

"No, I am Hasan Agib. El Tarabishi is my uncle. I am the one who writes the letters to you. My uncle cannot write."

Uncle Albert nodded and smiled as though this explained everything. "Ah, beautiful penmanship. Excellent command of the English language," he commended the young man.

But I was still confused. I was wondering if my presence, being a woman, was the root of the problem. Or did this have anything to do with the anti-British sentiment among the populace we had heard about? After all, it was only three short years ago that Egypt was granted independence from British rule, though the British still seemed very much in charge. Was the pin on the man's lapel the sign of some sort of independence cabal?

"Why can't my uncle visit your uncle?" I pressed. "It was all arranged. And we just crossed the whole market to find him."

The young man looked at the packages in our hands and nodded sympathetically. But before he could answer, the blockade behind him parted to let a weathered old man pass.

The man, stooped and walking with a cane, shuffled slowly up to my uncle. He addressed him in Arabic, bowed, and then motioned with his hands, as if to shoo my uncle away. Though I didn't understand what he'd said, the message was clear. Then the young man said something to the old man, and they seemed to argue for a few moments.

"What is he saying?" I asked.

"This is my uncle, El Tarabishi." *Ha! We were finally getting to the point!* "He says he is honored to have had you as a customer for so many years. He is grateful that such an important Efendi has come from across the big water to see him. He hopes you will continue to favor his humble shop until his strength fails him. But now you must leave," the nephew translated.

I might have imagined it, but a pained expression crossed the young man's face.

"It's probably best if I told you what has happened," he said with a heavy sigh. "My uncle's shop was broken into last night. The thieves made a big mess. He has no fez to give you. The fez he made for you was destroyed. Now he wants you to go away."

CHAPTER 4

My uncle and I stood dumbfounded for a few moments. Perhaps this robbery explained the strange behavior of the men. And yet, I felt as though something was not being said.

A man was watching us from under one of the stores' awnings. For a moment, his face caught the reflected light of the building opposite and what looked like a silver scar gleamed across his black eyebrow. I shivered and looked quickly away.

"Why are you sending us away?" I asked. Even if the shop was broken into, at least they could offer my uncle some tea. "Do you think our visit has brought bad luck to your uncle's shop?" I was considering possible reasons for the men's conduct.

The young man eyed me for a moment, as though assessing my question. "Come this way," he said without answering me. "I will show you the shortest way out of the market."

Suddenly, the desire to argue any further deserted me. We were in a foreign land. We didn't understand the local customs. It was time to leave, if we were not wanted here. After all, it was only a fez.

Uncle Albert gulped for a few more breaths, but he was lost for words. I could tell that he was terribly hurt, but could not be certain if that was because he was offended by the way he had been treated or because his supply of fezzes now looked to be on shaky ground.

Scores of questions exploded in my mind as I turned to follow the young man out of the lane. Was he really the fez-maker's nephew? Or was he just pretending to be? To what end? And yet, it made sense that he had been the one to correspond with Uncle Albert on his uncle's behalf, who clearly spoke only Arabic and, I had no doubt, was illiterate. Was this man our friend or enemy? *But that's silly,* I chastised myself. *Why would we be his enemies?* And was the story about the robbery true? We hadn't actually seen inside the shop. But why would these men make up such a story?

The nephew ushered us away and walked us through what felt like a labyrinth of lanes that grew increasingly narrower and dirtier. We passed under ramshackle balconies protruding menacingly over the lane, ducked beneath archways between houses, and threaded through alleyways so narrow and tall that no light penetrated.

Uncle Albert huffed indignantly next to me. His stride was getting shorter, and he was beginning to hobble.

"How much further?" I asked.

"Not too far now," the man said and glanced quickly in the distance behind us.

I wondered if he was leading us into a trap. But to what purpose? It was plainly obvious, given the amount of packages we were carrying, that my uncle had spent all his money already.

And I had the distinct feeling that we were being followed.

"What is going on?" I said at last as we entered another narrow lane. "Why was your uncle's shop robbed?"

The nephew shook his head. "No questions, please. The walls have ears and the windows have eyes."

"I saw someone like you at the museum," I pressed, ignoring his request. I was referring to his pin and wondered if he would understand my meaning.

"Please, no more questions."

Before I could protest, we unexpectedly burst out into a street with traffic and noise. Disoriented, I turned to look for Uncle Albert and slammed into a man. He grabbed me forcefully by the shoulders and I screamed.

"Caroline?"

"James!"

"What are you doing here?" James asked.

"I'm so glad I ran into you!" I cried and cast a glance at the man who had been escorting us.

"Is this man your friend?" our Egyptian escort asked, pointing at James.

I nodded and smiled.

"Then I leave you here," said the nephew. He turned to face Uncle Albert. "I apologize for all the trouble my uncle and I have caused you and your lady friend. I hope in time all will be forgiven." And with that, he melted into the crowd.

I threaded my arm through James and breathed a sigh of relief.

"What was that all about?" James asked, looking at the place in the crowd where the nephew had disappeared.

"I'm too confused to explain just at this moment," I said and leaned my head on his shoulder. "Let's wait until the hotel. Could we perhaps fetch a taxi?"

Safely bundled into a cab, I again wondered if the story about the robbery was a ruse. But what purpose would that serve? Neither the nephew nor the fez maker had asked us for money. And they had not led us into a trap, as I had feared. It appeared that all they had wanted was for us to leave straight away. Why?

"How did you come to do business with this fez maker?" I asked Uncle Albert on the way back to the hotel. He had recovered a bit from his ordeal and was able to speak again.

"A chap I used to know. He had a fez I rather admired. It had a scarab stamp inside—the maker's mark. And I thought, anyone with a beetle for a brand had to be good." *Infernal beetles, again!* "He does make exceptional fezzes," Uncle said and shook his head. "I wonder what I am to do now."

"I'm positive the concierge can suggest a reputable place. Plus, we can make an official complaint," I suggested.

"No," Uncle Albert said. "If the man's store has been robbed, we should not add to his troubles."

Given how he had just been treated, I considered my uncle's attitude towards the whole affair quite noble. I felt equal measures incensed and puzzled by the whole thing.

To James' credit, he did not ask for an explanation of our adventure before I was ready to give him one, but simply spent the ride back to the hotel looking at Uncle Albert and me with some puzzlement. We learned from him that he had been visiting the market for some gifts to take home.

At the hotel, the concierge, followed by a retinue of boys, rushed forward to help us with our packages.

"A successful morning?" the concierge asked, eyeing our packages. "We'll bring these up straight away."

I started to tell him about our adventure, but heeding my uncle's words, reconsidered. We proceeded to uncle Albert's rooms in silence. James followed us.

"I trust you had no trouble finding the fez shop, my lord, lady," said Wilford, my uncle's man, as we entered the suite.

"It was the most peculiar thing," my uncle said and sat down with a huff in an armchair. "I have the distinct impression that I was played at that market this morning."

"How so, my lord?" Wilford asked as he offered Uncle a refreshing drink on a salver.

Uncle Albert took a revitalizing draught. "The blasted fez place was robbed last night, and I've been cheated out of a fez!"

"Most peculiar, my lord," Wilford said, but did not show any further curiosity regarding the matter. "Which reminds me," he continued, "a package arrived for you while you were out."

Wilford brought forth a box wrapped in brown paper and tied with a string. "Shall I open it?" Wilford inquired.

My uncle nodded.

"Why, it's a fez!" Wilford exclaimed.

I grabbed the plain brown paper packaging. It bore no other markings except my uncle's name and the hotel.

"How extraordinary!" I exclaimed. "What could the meaning of this be?"

"Can someone fill me in on what happened at

the market?" James called out, unable to restrain his curiosity any longer.

I gave James and Wilford a quick account of our singular adventure.

"And is this fez from the same shop?" James asked.

Uncle Albert turned the hat over. "The silk is a new touch, but, yes, it bears the same mark. It's unmistakable, a scarab. See?" He handed the fez to James.

I looked over James' shoulder to the inside of the fez. The interior was lined with blue silk embroidered with golden scarabs. It was quite fetching.

"Why didn't they tell us they had sent a fez to the hotel?" I wondered out loud. "And why tell us that your fez was destroyed in the robbery?"

"I say," James cried out. "There is something tucked in here." He fished out a folded paper from behind the sweatband, which I had just taken to be a maker's label.

"Read it!" I implored.

"Dear Lord Tatham," James began reading, "if all has gone to plan, you have received this fez without much trouble. Forgive me for any rude behavior I might have shown you at the market. I am writing this note before our meeting, and have no idea how our meeting will proceed. Hopefully, you are unharmed." James stopped reading and looked up, quizzically. "I had the fez delivered to you," he continued reading, "while you were out. Forgive me again if I alarmed you during our meeting. I did not want our enemies to guess that I have given you the fez. My uncle's shop was broken into last night. Luckily, I had the fez in my possession, so the thieves did not find it. Please keep this fez safe. Don't tell anyone you have it. If your friend, the British archeologist, should discover a temple at Luxor, this fez will become very important. This is all I can write. I will follow up with more details at a later time."

"That's it?" I asked.

"That's it," James confirmed. "Let me see that fez again." He turned the hat in his hands and felt the lining. He handed it to me for inspection, but I couldn't detect anything hidden inside the fez either.

"This is mad!" James exclaimed. "I'm sorry, Lord Tatham, but I think your Egyptian friends have played a little joke on you."

"You think this is a joke?" I asked.

"Who would break into a fez shop to steal a hat?!" James countered. "Enemies? Secret messages? This can't be anything but a stunt." He smirked.

"But some of the story rings true," I said. As wild as the story sounded, I wasn't prepared to dismiss it entirely. "We did meet Mr. Hargrave— I assume he is the British archeologist the note refers to. And he does have a dig in Luxor."

"Yes, how did this nephew know about our chance meeting with Mr. Hargrave at the museum, I wonder?" James said.

Uncle Albert and Wilford were following our conversation with interest, but did not contribute.

"The pin!" I exclaimed. "The fellow next to the museum's director was wearing the same pin as the fez-maker's nephew. They obviously are part of the same group."

"What kind of pin?" James asked.

"A sort of scarab. A small, golden one," I said. "I wonder if it's some sort of political organization."

"I'll discreetly ask round about it," James said. "I have a few friends in the Foreign Office here."

We spent the rest of the day staring at the fez— interrupted only by a visit to Giza—but the hat did not surrender any of its secrets.

CHAPTER 5

As the day turned into evening, I reflected on the day's events. So outrageous were the adventures of the market, and the subsequent note, that I began to doubt their reality and they took on the quality of something out of a dream.

By next morning, in its proverbial cold light, I had completely dismissed the whole thing as a prank. I was still uneasy about it, and the joke really was done in bad taste, but I could find no other explanation of the peculiar events of the market and the fez.

Uncle Albert, however, had taken quite a different view of the whole affair. He had been quite calm about it all, and accepted the events at face value. He'd re-read the note, committed it to memory—a futile undertaking if there ever was one—and proceeded to burn the note and the packing paper. He then concealed the fez among his possessions and would not tell even me where he had hidden it. His commitment to the cause was such that he did not mention the incident to any of his fellow Royal Society members at dinner.

This morning we were departing on our journey up the Nile. Our luggage was taken away to the port, and we followed it soon after breakfast.

We traveled down by cars through the unequaled Cairo traffic. Donkeys carrying disproportionate loads, sellers pushing carts overflowing with colorful goods, stray animals, and throngs of men on foot, all vied for space on the road. Our driver made his way through the busy morning traffic using a series of sharp blasts from the car horn—to the sound of which all seemed impervious—accompanied by shouts and descriptive gestures. Kicking up a lot of dust and sand, the car wove its way towards our destination.

I found myself looking forward to this jaunt up the Nile river more than I had anticipated, or had allowed myself to admit. There was something romantic about sailing up this river of myths and legends as people had done for millennia in a *dahabiya*, the traditional Egyptian sailboat, eulogized by Victorian travelers, urged forward only by the power of the wind.

The previous day's visit to the Gaza monuments had left quite an impression on me. Next to the grandness of the pyramids, one could not help but feel insignificant. The stone monuments that had withstood human onslaught for thousands of years exuded awesome power and commanded respect. Exploring places that people had built thousands of years ago felt almost mystical. (Though the majesty of the experience was somewhat lessened by watching members of the Royal Society attempting to climb the Great Pyramid, each assisted by three Bedouins—two pulling up and one pushing from below).

In a land battered ceaselessly by sun and sand, the ancient Egyptian monuments stood stoic, permanent, and unmoved by the pitiful human condition around them. It was as though Egypt was a land of two parallel worlds: one belonging to the ancient gods and monuments—awe-inspiring and timeless; and the other belonging to men— corruptible, mortal and irrelevant.

It was the Egypt of the stone monuments that drew me in with a force I found myself unable to resist.

And yet, not all of Egypt's mysteries were on its surface. Mr. Carter, in digging up the Tutankhamen tomb, just three short years ago, had proven that the desert sands still held many secrets. How like an endless ocean the sands seemed. And just like the waters of the ocean, where wrecks lay half-forgotten at its bottom, so here tombs, replete with riches and treasure, lay buried deep beneath the sands. The sands of time had washed over them and swept them out of living memory.

We neared the port. The masts of the sailboats bobbed up and down lazily in the morning mist.

As we exited the car, I could see that Lord Mantelbury's secretary, Alistair Thomson, cousin of my dear chum Edwina Thomson-Brown, had arrived first, and some of the Royal Society's members were already gathered around him.

Lord Mantelbury, who'd felt that Alistair was not given as much responsibility within the Society as other members' private secretaries, had insisted that the task of securing a sailboat be assigned to Alistair. Much to Alistair's chagrin, I would imagine.

I would not normally take notice of Alistair —he was rather pale and ungainly—but he did seem to be hopping around quite anxiously at the moment. And his nervous dance was accompanied by lots of hand-waving on the part of the gathered members. From afar, the assembly looked like a ceremonial dance of some sort. I fancied that Alistair looked like a sacrificial victim and wondered vaguely if Alistair was about to be slaughtered and offered up to the gods.

Nearing the crowd, my heart gave an excited lurch. What misunderstanding had Lord Mantelbury's private secretary cooked up this time? Uncle Albert must have had a similar thought, because he hastened towards the gathering with a jaunty spring in his step.

"What do you mean we are traveling on a *Thomas Cook and Son* steamer?" The demanding voice of Lord Fetherly, laced with indignity, floated towards us on the breeze coming from the Nile.

Alistair mumbled something in reply.

"Now, leave the poor boy alone," Lord Mantelbury, Alistair's employer, was saying. But I could see that he was casting uncharitable glances in his secretary's direction. "I'm confident the accommodations he has secured for us would be quite sufficient for the purpose." His demeanor belied his words.

Lord Packenham huffed like a petulant child. "But I had my heart set on a ride on a dahabiya," he said and I expected him to stomp his foot.

I looked towards Uncle Albert to gauge his reaction, and was surprised to find that a smile had stretched across his face. "Capital. Capital," he was saying to himself. "The boy has done splendidly." He rubbed his hands.

For a moment, I wondered if Uncle Albert was simply excited to be traveling up the Nile in a steamer. But the true source of his excitement was soon revealed.

"Now, Dingo," he said, addressing Lord Fetherly, "pay up, you scoundrel. I've won fair and square. Didn't I say the boy was bound to cock up the whole thing? Oh, buck up, Alistair, my boy. Don't look so gloomy. Chalk it up to character-building," he said to the downcast secretary. Then, turning to me, he added in a hushed tone, "I'm rather surprised he managed to secure a boat for us at all. I'd quite expected to have to row up the Nile."

Concocting ridiculous wagers was a favorite pastime among the Royal Society members, and various five-pound notes exchanged hands. Faced with this explicit vote of no confidence, Alistair had by now adopted the air of a cat caught in a downpour, discovering the cat-flap locked.

"Do you know what's happened?" I asked James as I sidled up to him.

"Apparently, Alistair botched the booking in London. Realizing his mistake yesterday, he rushed to the Cook and Son's office, but the representative claimed that there were no dahabiyas left for hire. Apparently, the last dahabiya was secured by a rather domineering Englishwoman, according to the man at the office. To add insult to injury, with Americans having discovered Egypt, all private steamboats were fully booked, so the steamer Alistair has secured us a passage on is a public one—a Cook and Son tourist boat."

A pang of sympathy pinched the pit of my stomach. I suspected that the boat assignment had been a setup. The Lords knew perfectly well Alistair usually got terribly muddled. And it was rather unfair to have expected him to secure a passage up the Nile in any efficient manner.

Truth be told, however, although I had been looking forward to sailing on a dahabiya, on reflection, having other travelers on the boat with whom to share the burden of the Royal Society was not such a bad thing. The probability of having a conversation about anything other than beetles greatly increased with each non-member on the boat.

As more and more locals gathered around us demanding *bakshish*, it was decreed that a decision had to be made soon about the tourist steamer. The more ambitious among the members pointed out that a further delay to the beetle collecting tournament would be insufferable. And the more perceptive ones argued that the Society had to make its way to the dig in Luxor before Mr. Hargrave and his brother, Lord Chatfield, changed their minds.

Thus, faced with the inevitable, the members acquiesced to the plebeian cruise.

Our appointed boat's captain seemed to be growing impatient, saying something about a schedule, and began yelling instructions at the locals standing around. At this point, barefoot youngsters took a piece of luggage each, which caused some confusion among the Society's members, who thought that urchins were running away with their luggage. But matters were settled to everyone's satisfaction when it was explained that the boys were bringing the luggage on board.

My uncle and the rest of the chaps from the Royal Society had once again brought an inordinate amount of equipment, this time devoted to the collection of insects. From various nets (aerial, sweeping, clapping, aquatic and ones shaped like circular forceps), to all sorts of implements to dig, sift and examine sand, the porters were busy carrying boxes filled with, beating sheets, Berlese funnels, sieves, screen-bottom buckets, sticky traps, aspirators, jars, pins, and pocket exhibition boxes—which were like cigarette boxes but with a glass lid for showing off prized arthropod specimens, and quite the unwelcome thing to see at breakfast by the uninitiated.

Taking a leaf out of the book of Hakim Said Farrokh, the 12th century Persian scholar, the more intrepid of the members had brought along muslin tents. Not to be outdone, Uncle Albert boasted a set of loupes and hand-lenses made by the famed Dutch spectacles maker Zacharias Janssen—which he imagined made him the envy of the Royal Society—and which he flicked out whenever someone brought forth a pocket exhibition box.

But despite all the diverting insect paraphernalia, it was my uncle's new ballroom rug that elicited the greatest cries of excitement from the porters.

I nodded with appreciation. The adventure promised to be a fruitful one.

Uncle Albert and I proceeded to the boat. The steamer *Mentuhotep,* despite its clunky name, was not a bad-looking vessel. Long and elegant, with a white hull and mahogany decks, it sat gracefully on top of the Nile waters. As I let my eyes roam over the airy decks, and pictured myself taking in the sights while I sipped a gin and tonic under the awning on the upper deck, a man popped up at the railing.

"Hello!" he called down to us. "Lord Tatham, Lady Caroline!" He took off his hat and waved it. It was Mr. Hargrave, the archeologist.

CHAPTER 6

"Hello, Mr. Hargrave," I waved to him. "What a surprise!"

"Indeed, it is a pleasant one," he replied. "I'd quite given up hope of any friendly faces on the ship. Come on board," he said and disappeared from view.

We boarded just as Mr. Hargrave descended the sweeping staircase that gracefully curved down from the top deck. He made our introductions to the captain, Captain Saleeb, a local man in a crisp white uniform, and we proceeded up to the promenade deck to await the departure of the boat. From here we could watch the porters scurrying back and forth with trunks, boxes and crates under the watchful eyes of the valets.

"I must say," I began, as we reclined—Uncle Albert with some difficulty—on woven rattan loungers, "I'm surprised to see you here, on a tourist steamer."

"Why?" Mr. Hargrave asked. He had cleaned up quite well. Gone was the fine layer of dust, replaced by a linen morning suit in a light color. His dark hair was equally tidy, having been fetchingly slicked back, and his amulet must have been hidden somewhere deep under his shirt and tie. His new look was rather becoming.

Suddenly remembering James, I glanced around for him, but as I could not see him, I assumed he was helping Lord Packenham settle in. There was plenty of time for that, I decided. I was rather more curious to find out what Mr. Hargrave was doing on our boat.

"I would have expected you to have your own private schooner, Mr. Hargrave, or to at least take the train," I said.

"A private boat is quite an unnecessary expense, according to my brother," Mr. Hargrave answered. "An enormous outlay for staff, crew and upkeep. According to him, it's more sound to leave all of that to the professionals, like Cook and Son."

"But it must be a rather slow way to travel, especially on a tour steamer with all the stops it makes along the way," I countered. "Why not the train? I hear it's a great deal faster."

He nodded. "You are quite right, but my brother loathes the trains here. Cramped, hot and noisy. And I have to agree with him. We traveled down to Cairo on the train just the other day, and one races through the desolate countryside and sees nothing of the temples and the history of Egypt. It would probably not surprise you to learn that most of the ancient ruins are along the Nile."

I nodded. The maps inside my guidebook had made that quite clear.

"The two narrow green strips running alongside the river are the only fertile land in the whole country," Mr. Hargrave continued.

I nodded again. Lush palms lined the river banks, but I knew that just beyond lay a land of barren sand.

"And the Nile," he went on, "was the only way for the ancient Egyptians to transport building material for their grand projects. Traveling in a boat along the Nile is traveling like the pharaohs." He chuckled.

"Hear! Hear!" Uncle Albert enthused. And finding himself without the requisite drink, he motioned to one of the attendants for a tipple.

"Plus, the trip up the Nile gives me the opportunity to observe the land and landscape for any features that might signal hidden temples and burial grounds," Mr. Hargrave continued. "That's how I discovered our latest dig, observing it from the water. A peculiarity in the river bank, a dip, suggested an ancient causeway leading to a temple. Following that clue, we discovered a burial chamber dug deep into rocks further inland."

Our drinks arrived, and we paused for a moment. The ice in the glasses gave a satisfying clink.

While we'd been talking, a thwack, followed by a plop in the water, at regular intervals, had accompanied our conversation. As there seemed to be a lull in our chat, I got up and followed the source of the sound with my eyes. Leaning out and craning my neck to see above us, I spied the dark outline of a figure standing against the sun, swinging back and forth.

"Ah, I see you've discovered my brother, Eustace," Mr. Hargrave came by my side and followed my gaze, "or Lord Chatfield, as he prefers to be called. Allow me to introduce you to him."

Uncle Albert and I followed Mr. Hargrave up to the sun deck. There, Lord Chatfield was swinging a golf driver and sending golf balls into the water.

Only, upon closer observation, the pile of balls laying at his feet appeared to be not golf balls at all. These were stone scarabs! My uncle must have noticed this aberration as well, because he gave a slight start. But good breeding prevented him from commenting.

Mr. Hargrave winced as he noticed that we'd discerned the true nature of his brother's exercise.

"Eustace," his brother addressed the golfer, "allow me to introduce Lady Caroline Beasley and her uncle Lord Tatham. I've invited them, and all the members of the Royal Society for Natural History Appreciation, to visit us at the dig. Remember, I mentioned it. As luck would have it, they are to travel with us on this boat!"

Lord Chatfield turned, reluctantly, and greeted us without enthusiasm. A tall, serious man, he looked to be about a decade older than his brother. He was of the same dark coloring, but while the younger brother was quite handsome, the permanent scowl on Lord Chatfield's physiognomy made him look menacing. He was also entirely inappropriately dressed for the climate, or for golf. His black suit was of a severe cut, and I would not have been surprised if he wore a top hat to dinner. I wondered if he enjoyed Egypt at all.

"I don't know why you insist on bringing random people to the dig. It only slows down our work," Lord Chatfield said to his brother.

"They were friends of our late father," the younger brother countered with something akin to pleading in his voice. "Father was a member of their club, remember? I'm sure he would have insisted we invite them to the dig. And, anyhow, I'm in charge of the excavation," Mr. Hargrave concluded with more confidence.

"And I'm in charge of the purse-strings," his brother replied in a somber tone. "Don't forget, Nigel, that I finance your excavations. I can choose to shut down the dig whenever I want."

And with that, Lord Chatfield turned his back on us and launched the next scarab into the water, which sent a visible shudder through my uncle's arthritic body.

I reprised my earlier observations of the older brother. Lord Chatfield did not strike me as a chap who took an interest in, or even enjoyed, Egypt.

Given his choice of golf balls, he seemed to have quite a low regard for Egyptian antiquities. So what was he doing here, spending time at digs?

But my thoughts were derailed by Uncle Albert. I could feel him seething next to me.

"Young man," my uncle said with great indignation in his voice, "what you are doing is sacrilege!"

Lord Chatfield turned and eyed him for a few moments. "What? These worthless things?" he said with derision, kicking into the water some of the scarabs that had strayed from the pile. "They are like sand here. One digs them up faster than one can get rid of them. One particular pharaoh seems to have been carving them with the speed of Luther printing anti-papal pamphlets. What was his name, Nigel?"

"Amenhotep III," the younger brother replied in a subdued voice.

"Nigel says that this Hotep fellow had scarabs made out for all sorts of announcements— weddings, feasts, building works. Hundreds of them about. I had an expert evaluate these. Completely worthless." Lord Chatfield paused to pitch another scarab into the water. "In fact," he said, now turning to glare at his brother, "if we don't uncover something truly valuable soon, I'd be apt to withdraw my funding."

With a smirk, the deplorable Lord turned his attention back to his golf swing.

"It's a bad omen, that," Uncle Albert said to me in a low voice and shook his head.

It seemed my uncle was not the only person who found Lord Chatfield's behavior unacceptable. A man from the staff had paused for a moment to observe him. The look he threw the golf player was murderous. Noticing me gazing at him, the attendant quickly looked away and returned to polishing the deck's railings.

Lord Chatfield was not a likable man, I decided. It was as though he went out of his way to be unpleasant. At least, Mr. Hargrave spared us the awkwardness of apologizing on his brother's behalf.

The older brother turned to face us again, with a bullying glint in his eyes. "Nigel informs me our dig is the site of a legendary treasure. But I have yet to see any evidence of that." He scoffed.

"And a deadly curse," his brother added under his breath.

The newspapers had already alluded to the curse, but any further query into the nature of this treasure was interrupted by a woman's voice.

"Mr. Hargrave, you know perfectly well the ancient priests made up these curses to keep the gullible thieves out of the tombs," the voice chastised and was soon joined by a prim woman of no more than forty. "They are not real."

"Ah, Mrs. Babcock!" Lord Chatfield exclaimed without turning. "Who would we turn to to state the obvious if we didn't have you?"

The woman just smiled pleasantly. She appeared to be accustomed to this abuse.

Ignoring his brother, Mr. Hargrave said, "Allow me to introduce Mrs. Babcock, my very capable private secretary. She is an invaluable addition to our team and knows just as much about Egyptian history as I do. If not more." He smiled at her and gave her a quick bow of respect.

"Thank you, Mr. Hargrave," said Mrs. Babcock, "that is very kind of you to say."

Although she didn't look like the blushing type, I thought I detected a slight flush rising on her cheeks at the compliment.

I liked Mrs. Babcock. And not only because she was a woman in a profession dominated by men. She seemed quite calm and efficient. Her tailored two-piece suit and the tidy tendrils of her bobbed hair, even in the heat of Cairo, signaled that she was in possession of an organized mind. And if Mr. Hargrave praised her knowledge of Egyptology, then she was undoubtedly rather good.

Although she was quite a few years older than him, I suspected that she had a soft spot for her employer. I vaguely wondered what had happened to Mr. Babcock. A married woman was unlikely to be a secretary to a male archaeologist in Egypt, unless he was her husband. How had she ended up being Mr. Hargrave's secretary?

Just then, a racket on shore drew our attention.

A woman was running towards the boat, as quickly as her rotund body would allow her.

"Don't let the boat sail away!" she yelled.

CHAPTER 7

Holding on to a large hat that was threatening to fall off, the woman yelled again, "Stop the boat!"

An American, I concluded by her accent, and quite devoid of any decorum. The impression of crudeness was heightened by the presence of lots of colorful shawls and beads wrapped about her body, though a rather high quality dress was hidden underneath them. I identified some of the trinkets around her wrists and neck as those sold by local street vendors.

The vendors loitering along the pier must have recognized the provenance of the items as well, because they descended upon her with a gusto I had not observed before. One assumed, given their substantial experience, that the sellers could spot a patsy from miles away.

As shouts commending the virtues of various goods intermingled with cries for help, Uncle Albert shuffled next to me for a better view of the commotion. His presence brought my thoughts back to our experience at the Cairo market the previous day. The memory somewhat moderated my thoughts towards the woman on the shore.

Upon hearing her cry of desperation, one of the attendants from our boat finally came to her aid and drove away the gathered merchants with rough shouts.

The woman had left in her wake a trail of scarves, beads and whatnots, which was tracked by the porter boys carrying her trunks. Bringing up the rear was a slim young woman with mousy hair, with the look of a paid companion about her—plainly dressed and unassuming—who collected with a skittish hand the stray articles her employer had shed.

The captain appeared on the bridge. "Don't worry, madam, the ship will not depart without you," he called out to her. "Mrs. Gladstone, I presume," he said, and offered her his arm to lead her up the bridge.

"Thank you, my good man," the woman said breathlessly, and leaned on the offered arm. Then, staring at his face as though suddenly realizing that he was Egyptian, she faltered. One could observe the indecision, of whether to trust this foreigner, play out on her features. Inspecting his uniform, as if to confirm there was no artifice and that he was indeed the captain of the boat, she finally appeared to relent.

"And this young lady is your companion, Miss Parker, I presume?" the captain continued without showing any resentment towards the older woman. He was perhaps accustomed to such attitudes.

Miss Parker blinked at the captain and then looked around saucer-eyed, as though frightened by all she saw. She was jumpy and seemed alarmed by her surroundings. I wondered if she had traveled much or if this was her first time abroad.

"Hello, Miss!" Alistair's voice, coming from somewhere below me, greeted Miss Parker with an uncharacteristically sunny tone. The man himself then rushed down the bridge to meet the two women.

Miss Parker answered him with a shy smile. Alistair offered to help her with the items she had collected, but she refused rather abruptly, and he withdrew with a terrible blush blooming on his face.

That Alistair should know a young American maiden was completely out of character, and I made a mental note to ask him about it later. I wondered if we might get to witness a blossoming romance on this trip.

Having loaded all the trunks, Wilford came by and led Uncle Albert away while I remained on the deck for a few more moments. But as the attendants were giving every indication of the boat's imminent departure, I withdrew to my cabin to freshen up.

My room resembled much of the rest of the boat—walls and surfaces lined with dark wood paneling, trimmed with gold, and accented by quasi-Egyptian fixtures. But despite the dark wood, the cabin was spacious and so was the bed. I even had my own private bathroom with a ceramic tub. A large window afforded a view of the deck and the shore beyond. A couple of chairs and a little table were placed by the window, and I pictured myself taking morning tea here while enjoying the view as we glided past ancient sights.

The boat gave a lurch, and I looked out of my window to see the shore moving away from us. Barefoot children waved off the vessel from the edge of the bank. But it was an Egyptian man, standing under the shade of a palm tree to the side, that caught my attention. He gave a clear nod to someone on our boat, and as he did so, the scar across his eyebrow glinted in the morning sun.

It was the man from the market!

My mind jumped back to the narrow street where I had last seen him and then to the note I had dismissed as a joke. Perhaps I should not have disregarded it so quickly. The man's presence here could not be accidental. Had he followed us here? Who had he nodded to? One of the staff or someone else entirely? Perhaps I needed to keep a close eye on Uncle Albert and his fez.

I fished out the passenger list I had received upon boarding and located the names of all the Society's members and their secretaries on the register. Listed were also the two brothers whose excavation we would be visiting, their secretary, and the American woman I had witnessed boarding with her companion. If my tally was correct, there were just three other people I had yet to meet—Mr. and Miss Kershaw, I assumed father and daughter, both listed as archeologists, and a Mr. Dalton, an antiques dealer.

I lingered for a while in my room after I'd changed, collecting my thoughts. The note tucked inside Uncle Albert's fez had seemed to suggest that the fez contained information regarding something important to be found at Luxor. It had also alluded to Mr. Hargrave. I wondered if the presence of Mr. Hargrave and his brother on the boat was accidental. And why had Mr. Hargrave been so keen to invite the Royal Society to his dig? The note's writer, the fez-maker's nephew, seemed to consider Mr. Hargrave a friend. Then why had he not given the fez, or the information he seemed to think was hidden inside it, to Mr. Hargrave directly?

Was it a coincidence that everyone else on board, besides the Royal Society and the American woman, was somehow connected to Egyptian archeology?

They can't all be after Uncle Albert's fez!

I dismissed the idea as ludicrous and pushed the thought of the man with the scar from my mind. Perhaps it had been a trick of the light and I had imagined the whole thing.

Venturing into the lounge, where cold

lemonade and other refreshments were being served, I found Uncle Albert nodding off in one of the club chairs. The rest of the Royal Society had followed his example.

Just then, a woman about my age, with wild golden-brown hair and an air of confidence and independence, breezed in, followed by an older gentleman dressed in the fashion favored by Egyptian scholars of Anglo-American extraction— a khaki suit with a pith helmet.

They could be no other than Mr. and Miss Kershaw.

The woman's hair intrigued me exceedingly. Though unkempt, the style seemed to be deliberate, as though she was beyond such trifling things and had given in wholeheartedly to the heat and humidity of Egypt. I found her devil-may-care attitude terribly chic and avant-garde. Her clothes were equally nonchalant. Her flowing trousers were paired with a loose polka-dot shirt, and she had accessorized the whole ensemble with some local artisan jewelry. I would not have been surprised if it was of ancient Egyptian provenance.

Her languid movements under the flowing garments made her look as though she were floating around the lounge. Her skin was tanned to the point of almost matching her hair, which made her luminous blue eyes stand out even more. She seemed so at ease and even exchanged a few quiet words with the staff, perhaps in Arabic. The attendants were terribly impressed, I could tell.

While I held no self-deprecating views about my own beauty—my trim figure, blonde hair and bright smile had brought me many unwelcome offers of marriage—yet, suddenly, I felt dowdy and matronly in my morning dress.

"You are Lady Caroline Beasley," Miss Kershaw said without preamble. She had a deep and sultry voice that took me by surprise more so than her comment. "I have seen you in the society pages!"

I nodded modestly and smiled. And registered that Miss Kershaw was British.

"Yes, I remember," the young woman continued, "you ran away to the South of France to escape an engagement! And then when he followed you, you escaped to Italy. How wonderful!"

Ah, Cecil. I sincerely hoped I would not run into his mother, Lady Morton, in Egypt.

Quick introductions were made and after relating my association with the Royal Society, and the Society's current beetle mission, which was met with raised eyebrows, I invited Mr. Kershaw and his daughter to join me.

"I understand you are archaeologists," I said, moving the topic of discussion away from the intricacies of why I was my uncle's secretary. I didn't want to explain that while I was quite well off and did not need to work, I remained his secretary because I had become rather fond of

Uncle Albert. Plus, the work allowed me to spend time with James, to whom I was engaged, though not officially.

"That's correct," Mr. Kershaw answered. "I've lived in Egypt for over twenty years now. I became a widower soon after Margaret was born, so she has been by my side at excavations since she was a little girl." He patted her on the knee.

"Must have been terribly exciting," I said. And I meant it.

"It was a rather exciting way to grow up," Miss Kershaw said. "Running up and down pyramids and climbing ancient ruins. No better way to spend a childhood and develop the imagination. The whole of Egypt was my playground."

I gazed at father and daughter. There was so much resemblance between them—the untamed hair, the intelligent eyes. Mr. Kershaw's face, deep brown and weather-beaten, bore the evidence of spending twenty years under the Egyptian sun, perhaps even enduring the odd sand-storm.

"Are you headed to a dig up the Nile?" I asked.

I noticed a cloud pass over Mr. Kershaw's already dark face.

"It's a prickly topic with Daddy," Miss Kershaw said and smiled at her father.

I lifted an eyebrow.

"You see, my father can be quite abrasive sometimes. And while I was gone for a few years, to study archeology in New York, Daddy got into a terribly bad scrape."

Her father let out a groan.

"You will never get to manage your own site, Daddy, if you don't learn to control your temper," she chastised him playfully. "He does get rather excited over the smallest disagreement about dates or kingdoms," she turned to me. "He still hasn't learned that success in life is chiefly due to being a *good sport*."

I nodded.

"Margaret, I can't abide fools. When someone is misidentifying a relief of Horus and labeling it as from the time of Setnakht instead of Twosret, I need to speak my mind. Any fool could see that the glaze on those pot fragments was from the Nineteenth Dynasty, not the Twentieth." He sighed in an exasperated manner.

Mr. Kershaw's stubbornness reminded me of Uncle Albert when identifying an obscure beetle or orchid. The similitude endeared the father to me, but I could also sympathize with his daughter.

"Yes," Miss Kershaw shot back, "but you cannot call people fools. At least not to their faces. That's not the way to get your dig back."

I sensed that this was a rather regular topic of discussion between father and daughter.

Her father shook his head stubbornly. "Well, they are all fools. And now we have to put up with them on this very boat."

CHAPTER 8

As if on cue, Lord Chatfield walked in, followed by his brother and the secretary. Mr. Kershaw threw a murderous look in Lord Chatfield's direction, and I presumed we had ascertained the identity of the fool Mr. Kershaw had been referring to.

The daughter also shifted uncomfortably in her seat and cast a furtive glance towards the newcomers.

Lord Chatfield, for his part, also flung a dismissive glare in the Kershaws' direction and scoffed. His brother was more apologetic in his demeanor. Mrs. Babcock was the only one who behaved civilly and spared them a polite smile.

The tense but wordless exchange left me with the impression there was a long history between the Egyptologists and I looked forward to the story behind the animosity unfolding as we traveled up the Nile.

The silence in the room, however, was uncomfortable, and I was glad when the woman with the shawls, Mrs. Gladstone, rattled in. One of her shawls had found its way to her head, and it was now unbecomingly wrapped around her frizzy dark hair, in an attempt to emulate the latest fashion. She was followed by her companion, looking as uncomfortable as ever.

Introductions were again made, and as Mrs. Gladstone was the new addition to the company, and the only one without an archeological bone to pick, all attention shifted to her.

"And what brings you to Egypt, Mrs. Gladstone?" Miss Kershaw asked. "Are you traveling alone? Are you a widow?"

Mrs. Gladstone's rather garish outfit precluded her from being a widow, I would have thought.

"Mr. Gladstone is not much of a traveler," the woman answered in a loud voice, quite in line with her attire. "He's a financier, in New York, on Wall Street. We live in Manhattan," she added hastily. "He thinks traveling to Long Island is like going to a foreign country." She laughed at her own witticism.

"Is that far?" the secretary, Mrs. Babcock, asked.

"Oh, yes, dear. It is like a different country. All those grand houses and stables—" Mrs. Gladstone paused suddenly and glanced quickly at her companion. "And as I'm getting on in age," Mrs. Gladstone continued after a moment, "I decided to take matters into my own hands and travel a bit."

"Why Egypt?" Miss Kershaw pressed. "It's rather far and an ambitious trip to tackle for one who has not traveled much."

The boat jerked, and I noticed that several of the Royal Society's members were now awake, but whether that was due to Mrs. Gladstone's sonorous voice, or to the boat's activity, was difficult to say.

"I hope we haven't hit a sandbank," Lord Chatfield said and got up abruptly to speak to one of the staff.

"I like cats," Mrs. Gladstone said, and it took me a moment to realize that she was answering Miss Kershaw's question. "And I was visiting the museum in the park one day, the big one..."

"The Metropolitan Museum of Art?" Miss Kershaw suggested.

"That's the one. I'm not much of a museum goer, you see. And I was looking at their Egyptian collection, and I saw that they must have worshiped cats, since there were so many cat statuettes. And I said to myself, Ethel, this must be a good place to visit. A place that likes cats as much as I do."

And while several people rolled their eyes at the mention of cats as the reason to visit Egypt, most of the Royal Society's members nodded enthusiastically in agreement. And none as enthusiastically as Uncle Albert, who seemed engrossed in her story. I suspected that he had discovered a kindred spirit in Mrs. Gladstone.

Mrs. Gladstone's reasoning for her trip had left much of the room speechless, and only the clink of glasses arranged by the waiter behind the bar filled the silence.

Mr. Hargrave watched her with a particular air of annoyance. Or was it skepticism?

But it seemed that Mrs. Gladstone was not a woman who troubled herself by dwelling on the causes behind awkward silences. "I dabble in a bit of spiritualism as well, you see," she continued, unperturbed.

Miss Parker's face went ashen, and I wondered if the talk of spiritualism troubled her. At that moment, Mrs. Gladstone caught her companion's eye, and what looked like a warning passed between them.

Mrs. Gladstone cleared her throat. "Yes, well. I'm not very good at it yet," she said demurely. "Just learning how to summon spirits." She waved her hands about in the air, making her cheap bracelets jingle. "But I now have my own spirit guide, and she told me that Egypt is the place to visit. So many ancient spirits floating about, you see. She's from ancient Egypt. So I thought, why not visit the young woman's birthplace? She was a slave—"

"If she was a slave in Egypt," Mr. Kershaw interrupted impatiently, "her birth place is unlikely to have been here."

"Well, now. Actually," Mr. Hargrave began, but a quick shake of the head from Miss Kershaw put an end to his objection. I wondered how well they knew each other and whether Miss Kershaw shared her father's dislike of Lord Chatfield and his brother.

"Poppycock," a deep voice announced from the doorway, and I presumed we were joined by the last member of this little party, the antiques dealer.

"Ah, Mr. Dalton," Mr. Hargrave said in a disparaging tone.

Mr. Kershaw also threw the new arrival an unkind glance. Whatever their disagreements about pottery glaze might be, it seemed the archaeologists concurred in their opinion of Mr. Dalton. I wondered why he didn't like him.

"What are you doing here, Dalton?" Lord Chatfield addressed the new arrival. "You're not allowed near my dig," he warned him.

I turned to watch Mr. Dalton's reaction. A lazy smile spread across his face from under his thick mustache. And despite being middle-aged, he still had a full head of hair, only slightly grizzled at the temples. His height rivaled that of Lord Chatfield and the two men glared at each other at eye level for a moment.

Mr. Dalton's athletic build was enhanced by a well-cut suit, and his expensive accessories—with a touch of crocodile skin—seemed to suggest quick money.

"It's a free country," Mr. Dalton said at last with an American drawl. "Well, it is now. Now that the Egyptians got some sense and kicked your government out." He smiled. "I'm sure the rest of the territories under British control will come to their senses soon enough."

"Is that what your German friends are telling you?" Lord Chatfield almost spat out the question.

Mr. Dalton's comment, however, had upset the sensibilities of the Royal Society, who stirred as one and got all in a fluster trying to defend King and Empire.

"Sorry to have caused offense, gentlemen," Mr. Dalton said, addressing the Royal Society. "I like yanking Eustace's chain from time to time. I meant no harm. I'm a big fan of the Empire. I have a lot of clients back in the States who pay a pretty penny for antiques from the old country. And items with aristocratic provenance, especially. Here is my card," he said and handed out his credentials to each of the Lords, who received them with a look of bewilderment. "If you ever want to offload some old knick-knacks gathering dust in the old castle, give me a holler on the blower, as you Brits say." He chuckled. "American colleges—universities to you —in particular, go out of their way to acquire the old-world, old-money, British-Empire look."

Mr. Dalton then walked up to the bar and ordered a drink. He leaned on the polished counter and took a sip. "But back to you, old boy," he said, turning to Lord Chatfield. "I have other connections in the area I want to visit. And you can't stop me." He raised his glass as if to toast Lord Chatfield, but the gesture was full of contempt.

"I've warned my men to keep an eye out for you. The foreman will make sure that nothing leaves the dig and the workers will not sell you anything," Lord Chatfield said in a threatening voice.

Mr. Dalton simply laughed in reply. The announcement of lunch prevented any further discussion.

Lunch proceeded in an awkward silence and it became evident that unless one wanted to hear more about Mrs. Gladstone's cats or slave girl, or the Royal Society's beetles, there was not much conversation to be had. The two camps of archeologists—Lord Chatfield and his brother, and the Kershaws—refused to speak to each other, while both ignored Mr. Dalton.

As the days on the water passed by, our company fell into an uneasy rhythm.

The Lords of the Royal Society strewed their insect paraphernalia across the decks—each member staking out a different part of the ship —to the detriment of the rest of the passengers. More than once, Mrs. Gladstone found her shawls or beads entangled in the nets cast across the sun deck to catch anything airborne that was foolish enough to make its way across our boat. Matters were not much improved by the presence of Uncle Albert's carpet, which, due to its sheer size, could not be safely stowed away. The carpet was moved to a different location each day, presumably to be out of the way, but invariably it tripped up Mrs. Gladstone, whose rounded middle impeded a clear view of her feet.

For her part, Mrs. Gladstone set up shop in the ladies' salon—much to the annoyance of Miss Kershaw—where she insisted on contacting ancient Egyptian spirits at all times of the day. The sessions also caused evident distress to Miss Parker, who looked annoyed and worried by the practice in equal measures. I wondered why a woman who was so opposed to spiritualism would take up employment with someone like Mrs. Gladstone.

I was rash enough to make a remark along those lines in the presence of Mrs. Babcock one afternoon.

"Perhaps women of little means can not be too selective about employers," she rebuked me. "You may well wonder why I remain in the employment of Mr. Hargrave, despite Lord Chatfield's character. After my husband's death, the Hargraves were generous enough to offer me this position and pay my son's school fees."

Mortified by my inconsiderate comment, I avoided Mrs. Babcock for some time after that.

It seemed that the beauty of the countryside which glided past us was lost on most of the passengers: the archaeologists, in fear of running into each other, kept to their rooms; the Royal

Society's private secretaries were preoccupied with recording the daily insect catch; and Mrs. Gladstone rarely left the ladies' lounge.

As I had relinquished my beetle-counting duties to Wilford, who found the cruise unvaried and welcomed the diversion of the task, I often spent quiet afternoons up on the sun deck. With the white curtains, drawn against the sun, fluttering in the soft breeze, I observed rural Egypt float by—the lush date trees, the farmers laboring by hand in the fields, the crumbling villages which appeared to be under constant threat of being swallowed up by the desert sands, and the odd ancient Egyptian monument dotting the landscape in the most incongruous way.

The cruise, however, exerted a strange force on one group—it put the Lords of the Royal Society in a pensive mood. After the moth traps had been set up for the night, they would sit in the lounge, reminiscing into the late hours of the night about their youth and about making the slow journey to India to take up their government posts.

Uncle Albert—saying that his head was the safest place for it—had taken to wearing his new fez, and I secretly hoped that the fez would vanish and then we would have a mystery on our hands to add some excitement to our idle days on the water. Each morning, however, Uncle Albert appeared at breakfast with the fez secured resolutely on his head.

Yet, the unhurried days were not without reward. I learned through the inevitable gossip that permeated our closed society that Mr. Kershaw's dislike of Lord Chatfield and his brother stemmed from the belief, perhaps mistaken, that they had machinated against him to snatch away the dig site at Luxor. And as his flashy ways had suggested, Mr. Dalton was rumored to be involved in shady dealings with Egyptian antiques. Perhaps his transgressions would have been overlooked if there weren't quite so many Germans among his clients. I vaguely wondered if Mr. Dalton was a spy.

But it was Lord Chatfield slipping on a stone scarab left carelessly on the promenade deck, and almost pitching over the railing into the Nile, that brought my mind back to the purported curse and treasure of his dig.

CHAPTER 9

On the fifth day, after leaving behind the ancient tombs of Beni Hasan, and after Lord Chatfield had slipped on a stone scarab—quite ominously, according to Uncle Albert—I could not restrain my curiosity any longer.

I decided to broach the subject of the dig at Luxor, and specifically the legend of the treasure Lord Chatfield had alluded to.

We had four more days ahead of us before we reached our next destination, Dendera, and then Luxor, so any animosity my question was bound to stir up was preferable to the fraught silence, broken only by the inane discussions of the Royal Society's members over the ideal length of tibia on a dung beetle required to transport a dung ball, three-quarters of an inch in diameter, up the steep gradient of a sand dune.

I brought up the question while we had all gathered in the lounge in the late afternoon, for drinks before dinner. The waiters bustled between the bar and the guests scattered on the Chesterfields and club chairs. The polished wood paneling sparkled in the afternoon sun. My own seat gave me a good view of the room.

"Lord Chatfield," I said, swirling a Martini, "tell me more about your dig at Luxor. Is it a very significant find?"

"Why, yes," he said and cleared his throat. "Of course. Yes. It's very important. It's as significant as the tomb Mr. Carter came upon, if not more so, I daresay." He glanced towards his brother as though asking for assistance, and I got the impression that his lordship was not quite well versed in the details of the dig.

The statement about Mr. Carter's tomb was rather provocative, and both Mr. Hargrave and Mrs. Babcock shifted uncomfortably in their chairs.

"Come now, man!" Mr. Kershaw countered immediately, slamming down his glass, splashing some gin about. "You don't know what you are talking about. Greater than the Tutankhamen tomb! Such a load of—"

"Mr. Kershaw!" Mrs. Babcock exclaimed. "Language! There are ladies present."

Mr. Kershaw looked about him mutinously. "Well, it just shows you how little Lord Chatfield knows about the Tutankhamen tomb. And Egyptology in general. A tomb greater than the one Carter found! Ha!" He shook his head and took up his drink.

"That's not how you felt about this particular site when the Department of Antiquities took it away from you!" Lord Chatfield cried out with some glee.

"Perhaps I can offer some explanation, Lady Caroline," Mr. Hargrave jumped in. "While my brother does not mean to belittle the Tutankhamen find, what he means, I am sure, is that our dig offers something vastly different, and altogether perhaps more interesting to scholars."

He paused and looked at Mr. Kershaw to see if he was threatening to oppose him, but it appeared that Miss Kershaw had managed to subdue her father for the time being.

"The tomb we are excavating," Mr. Hargrave continued, "is from the Eighteenth Dynasty, and belongs to a man named Ahmose, who was a high priest at the temple of Amun-Ra at Thebes, which is present-day Luxor. Ahmose was the son of the pharaoh Amenhotep II, and became a high priest during the reign of his brother, the pharaoh Thutmose IV.

"Of course, the Eighteenth Dynasty, which was the first dynasty of the New Kingdom, is now best known for Tutankhamen. But the Eighteenth Dynasty was also a time of great splendor at Thebes, which was the capital of Egypt at the time, and the city we now know as Luxor was built on top of it. Thebes was the gateway to the Valley of the Kings and was also believed to be the dwelling place of Amun-Ra, the ancient Egyptians' supreme god. Now, it's interesting to note that initially Amun was just the local god of Thebes, the patron deity of the city, but beginning with the Eighteenth Dynasty, whose rulers hailed from Thebes, Amun was fused with the sun god Ra to become Amun-Ra. Incidentally, Amun is alternatively spelled with an 'e', and when Tutankhamen came to power, he amended his original name, Tutankhaten, by adding an 'amen' to proclaim his allegiance to the cult of Amun, or Amen...our English language is truly insufficient to capture the Egyptian pronunciations...You can tell how pharaohs tried to associate themselves with the god Amun through their names—we have Tutankh*amen* and *Amen*hotep I through IV—"

Someone gently coughed, interrupting the monologue.

"Right, yes," Mr. Hargrave said, but looked confused as to what to say next.

The members of the Royal Society, who had long ago lost interest in the archeologist's talk of pharaohs and deities, were currently engaged in an off-shoot discussion of Egyptian moths.

"You are quite wrong, Lord Mantelbury," Lord Packenham was saying. "The Sphinx moth, *Sphinx ligustri*, while named for this most illustrious of artifacts of ancient Egypt, is not native to Egypt at all. Which you would know if you ever read the 10th edition of *Systema Naturae* by Linnaeus." He let out a soft, derisive chuckle.

The conversation the Royal Society was conducting was only marginally less interesting than Mr. Hargrave's homily, but as I was the one who had asked about the tomb at Thebes in the first place, I turned my attention back to the archeologist.

"Get on with it, man," Mr. Kershaw said impatiently. "Get to the point. What of this treasure everyone in Cairo has been hinting about?!"

I gave a silent thanks that Mr. Kershaw had verbalized what I had been thinking.

"Right, getting back to our man, Ahmose. Now, his brother, the pharaoh Thutmose IV, is perhaps best known for having spiritual visions and erecting the Dream Stele you saw standing in the paws of the Great Sphinx of Giza."

"Oh, I remember reading about that," said Alistair unexpectedly, and cast a shy glance in Miss Parker's direction. "Thutmose, who was not in line for the throne, came to power after he was visited in a dream by the Sphinx."

"Yes," Mr. Hargrave said. "At the time, the Great Sphinx of Giza was buried up to its neck in sand. So Thutmose dug out the statue, as his dream had instructed him, and later, when he became the pharaoh Thutmose IV, he placed a tablet of thanks at the Sphinx's feet. But any guidebook can tell you that. What is not so well known is that his brother, Ahmose, was also prone to spiritual visions."

"Ah, yes," Mrs. Gladstone jumped in. "The ancient Egyptians were very spiritual beings.

I contacted several Egyptian princesses and priestesses over the last few days."

"No cats?" Mr. Dalton asked maliciously and smirked.

Mrs. Gladstone's face turned red, and she just glared at him.

By this point, most of the listeners had started fidgeting in their seats and calling out to the waiters for more drinks. Mr. Hargrave was in danger of losing the attention of his audience, despite the promise of a tale of treasure.

His secretary, Mrs. Babcock, must have noticed the brewing mutiny. "Mr. Hargrave," she said, "perhaps getting directly to the treasure would be more interesting for the lay members of our group."

She smiled timidly at him, as though worried her comment would be met with a reprimand.

But the young archaeologist accepted the suggestion without any visible malice. "Yes, you're quite right, Mrs. Babcock. Now, to understand the significance of our find, you have to know a little bit about the sun god, Ra. As an aside, and this would interest you, Mrs. Gladstone, the god Ra created the god Bastet, which took the form of a cat."

Mrs. Gladstone smiled and looked about the room in a self-satisfied way, as though all her talk about Egyptian cats was vindicated.

"In any case," Mr. Hargrave continued, "the

ancient Egyptians believed that the god sun Ra took on different forms as he made his progress across the sky—falcon, ram. But it's the beetle form we are interested in, which is the form Ra assumes at sunrise."

At the mention of a beetle, the whole Royal Society looked up and took notice.

Mr. Hargrave smiled. "Up until we discovered the tomb of Ahmose," the archeologist continued, "and this will interest the Lords of the Royal Society in particular, it was believed that this beetle form of Ra, called *Khepri*, did not have its own cult."

This deficiency caused a murmur of dissent to pass through the Royal Society.

"Though one sees drawings and carvings depicting Khepri as a beetle in every tomb," Mr. Hargrave resumed his narrative, "no temple was known to be dedicated solely to Khepri." He made a dramatic pause, and the Royal Society was hanging on his word. "But with the discovery of the tomb of Ahmose, we are now certain that a cult of Khepri existed in Thebes."

"If such a cult existed," Mr. Kershaw interrupted, "it would've been kept secret. It would not have been a state-sanctioned cult."

"That's correct," Mr. Hargrave agreed. "From inscriptions, we deduced that Ahmose had visions of Ra in beetle form, and went on to establish a secret cult of Khepri. That is why we traveled to

Cairo, to let the Department of Antiquities know about it and to discuss the need for further digs in the area."

The mention of further digs made Mr. Kershaw frown.

"If I am understanding you correctly, young man," Uncle Albert piped up, "you are saying that you have discovered a cult that worshiped beetles."

Mr. Hargrave nodded. "In a manner of speaking."

A joyful buzz emanated from the Royal Society's end of the lounge.

"But why dedicate a whole cult to a beetle?" Mrs. Gladstone asked, incredulous. Judging by their glares, the Lords were not happy with her query.

"That's an excellent question," Mr. Hargrave said, oblivious to the feelings of the Royal Society on the subject. "Khepri, the beetle, symbolizes new beginnings and rebirth. He brings forth the sun from the underworld, heralding a new day. The ancient Egyptians saw a similarity between the dung beetle rolling a dung ball across the sand and the movement of the sun across the sky. To them, the dung beetle was a representation of Ra, and was sacred."

With each utterance about beetles, the members of the Royal Society stood a little taller in their club chairs, chests a little more puffed out.

"So what's so special about the tomb you discovered? Have you found the treasure yet?

Is every surface covered in gold, like in the Tutankhamen tomb?" Mrs. Gladstone's dark eyes sparkled like beetles.

Mr. Hargrave shifted in his seat, but was interrupted by his brother before he could answer.

"No, madam, the tomb we discovered is mostly covered in beetle carvings," Lord Chatfield said, unable to hide his disappointment. "But there is a reference, or so my brother assures me, to a temple devoted to Khepri containing riches beyond belief." He suppressed a laugh.

Then, as though suddenly becoming aware of the presence of Mr. Dalton, Lord Chatfield sent him a warning glare for good measure.

"Well, the ancient inscriptions could be interpreted several ways," Mr. Hargrave added cautiously. "They talk alternatively of a great treasure hidden inside the temple of Khepri, or an artifact of great power—one that can restore life and resurrect the gods themselves."

"Imagine that," Mrs. Gladstone said. "I wonder if it can bring back my dead cat."

Mr. Dalton choked on his whiskey.

CHAPTER 10

Mr. Hargrave's unexpected proclamation gave everyone pause, and for a few moments all guests seemed lost in thoughts of what this great treasure might be.

I was equally intrigued. Was this treasure what the fez-maker's nephew had alluded to in his note? Was he expecting Mr. Hargrave to discover this lost temple? And what information did Uncle Albert's fez contain?

Could the scarab pins on the lapels be a reference to this ancient cult of Khepri? Were the wearers seekers or defenders of the treasure? And who were these enemies the note had mentioned?

"But you haven't discovered this temple?" Mrs. Gladstone asked prosaically.

"Not yet," Mr. Hargrave conceded.

"So you've discovered nothing," Mr. Kershaw said and laughed. Miss Kershaw scowled at her father.

"We are exploring the area around the tomb for the temple," Mr. Hargrave said rather testily, losing his temper for the first time.

"Who would want to resurrect ancient deities?" Lord Packenham objected. "Of what use is that?"

"Use your imagination, man," Mr. Dalton countered forcefully. "Don't you see? These inscriptions Mr. Hargrave discovered must be referring to the original philosopher's stone."

James barked out a laugh. "You can't believe in the philosopher's stone, surely?" he asked, trying to contain his mirth.

"Why not?" Mr. Dalton said calmly. "The Egyptians believed in resurrection and the afterlife. That's why they made all these tombs and mummies. The scarab was the symbol of rebirth. My money is on a stone scarab that has some healing powers. Think about it—an ancient stone, lost to the ages. The philosopher's stone. And in any case, I don't have to believe it. But I have clients who would be willing to pay a pretty penny for such a stone."

"Is money all you are interested in?" Mr. Hargrave said.

"I'm a dealer and a pragmatist. I don't believe in this mumbo jumbo, but I'm not opposed to selling gullible people such trinkets," said Mr. Dalton, and looked directly at Mrs. Gladstone.

She just snorted.

"You may scoff, Mrs. Gladstone," Mr. Dalton said, "but the people who buy my artifacts are no less gullible than people who attend seances and contact mediums."

Mrs. Gladstone flushed uncontrollably. "I will have you know that the profession of the medium is very respectable and the methods are proved by scientific evidence." She huffed, as though her anger was making her short of breath.

Miss Parker touched her lightly on the hand, which made Mrs. Gladstone sit back and exhale audibly.

"Perhaps," Mrs. Gladstone said after a few moments, having regained some of her composure, "I could show you all what I mean in a little seance. I have been taking lessons with the most famous medium in New York—"

Her companion tapped her lightly again.

Mrs. Gladstone looked at her, but did not heed her warning. "Don't worry, Daisy," she said, "I know what I'm doing."

But as several people declined the offer of a seance, the topic was dropped.

I, for one, was quite disappointed. I would have thoroughly enjoyed a little seance. Not because I believed in such things, but because I wanted to see how skilled Mrs. Gladstone was really at manipulating her audience.

Undeterred by Mrs. Gladstone's interruption, Mr. Dalton returned to his topic of Egyptian artifacts.

"I think you'd be surprised to know that some of my best clients for Egyptian antiques are American colleges," he said to no one in particular. "Several of the oldest and most revered universities have secret societies with rituals based on those of ancient Egypt. They pay good money for valuable artifacts."

"Really?" I said. It was a rather interesting topic.

He nodded. "There is the Skull and Bones at Yale University, whose meeting place resembles an Egyptian tomb, the Sphinx at Dartmouth College, whose members meet in a tomb and carry canes emblazoned with Egyptian symbols, then there is the Sphinx Head at Cornell, and the Scarabbean Secret Society at the University of Tennessee, with members known as Scarabs. And these are just some of the better known ones."

"But not just universities," Miss Kershaw said. "Many of the so-called secret societies throughout history have been influenced by ancient Egyptian beliefs—the Knights Templar and the Freemasons, to name but a few."

"Oh, do you have any Freemasons among your customers?" Mrs. Gladstone asked Mr. Dalton eagerly.

Mr. Dalton looked pleased by the question. "I cannot reveal my clientele. I operate under the strictest confidence. That's why I'm so respected in this business."

Mrs. Gladstone nodded while Mr. Kershaw snickered.

"Ha! Respected—"

"Father," his daughter said, cutting him off

with a note of pleading in her voice. "Not now."

"All I'll say is that Mr. Dalton has some questionable customers," her father added defiantly. "Those Germans, and even some of Mussolini's Italians."

"It's true that many men from history have been fascinated by the Egyptians," Mr. Dalton said, without rising to the bait. "Why, even the Roman emperors brought back symbols of Egyptian power to Rome."

"Yes, unfortunately, the treasures of Egypt have been ransacked for centuries," Mrs. Babcock said with a sigh. "Many tombs have been robbed bare, and the contents sold off to dealers." She glared pointedly at Mr. Dalton.

"Like you don't strip them bare," he objected and smirked.

"Mr. Dalton!" Mrs. Babcock protested. "We are scholars! Everything is recorded and cataloged. We donate all the items we find to the Cairo museum!"

"That's not what I've heard," he said.

Mrs. Babcock and Mr. Hargrave raised vehement objections in unison.

"Stand down, stand down. I'm just yanking your chain," Mr. Dalton said and laughed. I could tell he derived pleasure from stirring trouble.

"And what are you hoping to find at Luxor, Mr. Dalton?" I asked, intrigued by the accusations cast his way.

"Oh, you never know what will appear. I have a client who is very interested in what might come out of Mr. Hargrave's supposed temple. If he ever finds it, that is." Mr. Dalton cast him a teasing glance. "Very interested in reincarnation and such, my client. Fancies himself a bit of an alchemist."

"But if this resurrection stone is really discovered," Alistair interjected, "it would be quite something."

"That's an understatement, my boy," Mr. Dalton said, and took a leisurely sip out of his whiskey while looking at Lord Chatfield over the rim of his glass.

"Whatever is discovered in the temple is bound to go to the museum in Cairo," Miss Kershaw objected.

"Perhaps they would not be interested in it," Mr. Dalton said with a shrug. "If the rumors are true, my wealthy client is prepared to pay a lot of money for this stone. I doubt even Monsieur Lacau of the Department of Antiquities would object to selling it. After all, if it's just a stone scarab, as I expect, he might not need another one." A sly smile spread across his face.

"True. Those scarabs are like sand," Lord Chatfield said, returning to his thesis from earlier.

Mr. Hargrave groaned. "Each of those scarabs you lob into the water took ages to find," he protested, raising his voice. "They hold valuable information about an ancient culture. Each provides us with another clue to piece together this fascinating civilization. Even a fragment can hold precious knowledge."

Lord Chatfield rolled his eyes in a mocking fashion and took another sip from his drink. He was about to say something, but stopped himself. Then sat seething for a few moments, his eyes glaring.

Suddenly, he slammed down his tumbler on the table beside him and jumped to his feet. "I tell you what," Lord Chatfield said to his brother. "I'm going to prove to you that it takes no effort at all to find something of supposed value in Egypt. All one has to do is dig a bit. Takes no special skill." He looked around like a person possessed. "Yes, we can stop the boat right now and I'll go to shore and show you."

"Sit down, Eustace," his brother said, "you are drunk. We can't stop the boat."

"Nonsense!" Lord Chatfield waved his brother's objections away and swayed a bit. "I'm going to get the captain to stop the boat right now."

"Lord Chatfield, is that prudent?" Mrs. Babcock said. "There are other people on the boat."

"I'm certain none of the guests have any objections," Lord Chatfield said, looking around the room. "I daresay the Lords of the Royal Society are fond of the odd flutter. What do you say, gentlemen, should we wager a few bob?"

All the Lords nodded in unison. They looked

like penguins lining up at the zoo for their ration of fish from a bucket.

"I object," Mrs. Gladstone said with determination, making her beads jingle. "I don't want the boat to stop."

"I fear, madam, that you have been overruled," Lord Chatfield said and smirked while eying my uncle and his chums.

"I'll make sure Cook and Son hear about this irregularity," Mrs. Gladstone continued.

But it looked as though all the other guests were up for a bit of fun. As this stretch of the river offered no sights, Lord Chatfield's little escapade made everyone excited. The more industrious of the private secretaries already had their black notebooks out, talking odds and spreads.

In the commotion, one of the attendants must have called the captain. All the noise died down as he walked in.

"My Lord," Captain Saleeb turned to Lord Chatfield, "one of my crew has informed me that you'd like to stop the boat for an excursion to the shore. It is highly irregular and I cannot authorize it."

The two men stared each other down for a few minutes.

"If there was any other way," the captain said, "if this were a private sailboat, I would have no objections. But as matters stand, my hands are tied. I am answerable to Cook and Son."

"The lads have already taken our bets," chirped one of the Lords.

"Listen now, my man," Mr. Dalton also intervened. "I'm sure no one here objects to seeing Lord Chatfield make a fool of himself. Let him have his fun. And we'll have some fun as well."

Lord Chatfield was huffing and growing red in the face. The captain looked as though he was searching for a solution to avoid a row.

"Consider the dangers, my lord," the captain tried to reason with Lord Chatfield, who just waved the objection away.

I wondered vaguely what the dangers might be. Were there robbers who waited in the shadows to attack any foolish tourist who might venture ashore in the evening?

"However," the captain continued, "it would be inauspicious to continue our trip under the cloud of an argument. Perhaps I could send one of the boys to convey you to shore."

I wondered why the captain had relented. Perhaps he had instructions to make guests happy and give in to eccentric English requests. Or perhaps Lord Chatfield was well-connected enough back in Cairo to cause trouble for the captain.

"Excellent!" Lord Chatfield exclaimed. "Then it's settled. Get the dinghy ready."

"Eustace," Mr. Hargrave began, "this is silly. You don't have to prove anything. To me or to anyone."

But Lord Chatfield just downed another glass of champagne. "No, little brother," he said, "my mind is made up."

"Lord Chatfield," Mrs. Babcock said, "is it wise to go on shore in your state?"

"Nonsense, I'm perfectly fine."

As it was apparent that Lord Chatfield had had just enough to drink to make him argumentative and unyielding, his brother and secretary stepped aside as he charged through the door.

We all followed him and stood on the deck as the boat rowed away. Within moments, Lord Chatfield, pith helmet securely on, was at the bank. He waved to us, and we all waved back.

Though the sun had just set, there was still light enough to see Lord Chatfield on the shore.

He took out some sort of digging utensil and attacked the river bank.

"I say, is not twilight the feeding time of the Nile crocodile?" Lord Dodsworth asked, turning to the other Lords.

He had just finished asking his question when there was a splash in the water.

CHAPTER 11

The water churned wildly, and it took me a few moments to realize that Lord Chatfield was struggling just below its surface.

"Has he fallen in?" Mrs. Gladstone said, leaning over the railing precariously and peering at the shore.

"What's going on?" asked some of the shortsighted Lords.

"Does he need help?" asked those whose sight was superior.

On the deck below us, the crew seemed to have a better idea of what was happening, because they were yelling in Arabic quite animatedly at the boy in the rowboat. Exclaiming, he started to row back towards us frantically.

"He needs help!" Mrs. Gladstone was yelling as loud as the Egyptians. "Why is that wretched boy rowing away? Go back, go back I tell you." She gesticulated at the boy in the boat as though to make him turn back and help Lord Chatfield.

I returned my gaze to the frothing water by the shore and noticed, with horror, that the surface had suddenly turned calm. A serrated tail slid across the water, but in a moment that was gone too. Only Lord Chatfield's pith helmet bobbed silently on the water.

The deck below us was still quite agitated, and the cries of the men did not die down until the boy was pulled safely back on board.

Our deck, in contrast, had grown silent. Only Mrs. Gladstone kept insisting that someone should be sent back to the water to search for Lord Chatfield. The rest of us appeared to have read the warnings in our guidebooks.

We waited for quite some time on the deck, peering desperately into the murky waters of the Nile, hoping to see Lord Chatfield come out, but to no avail.

Captain Saleeb had joined us by now. "It's too dangerous to send out a search party," he said, confirming our fears. "The blood would attract other crocodiles to the area. We cannot risk another life." He then left to contact the authorities in Cairo and Luxor and inform them of the accident.

One by one, we made our way back to the lounge. The attendants served stiff drinks to all. And while most of us were distressed by the accident, none was more so than Lord Chatfield's brother.

He walked about the room like a caged tiger. "What can be done? We must do something. We must save my brother."

"I say! Buck up and all that," said one of the Lords, in an ill-advised attempt to be helpful. "Nothing we can do for him now."

"How could I have agreed to let him go on shore?" Mr. Hargrave continued, talking to himself, oblivious to all around him. "I, who knew what dangers the waters hold!"

"Don't be so hard on yourself, Mr. Hargrave," said Mrs. Babcock in a motherly tone. "He was a strong-willed man and he would not listen to reason once he had an idea in his head."

Mr. Hargrave nodded, but I doubted he had heard Mrs. Babcock.

I looked about the room.

"What are the chances he has survived?" asked Alistair.

"Very small, according to the latest volume of *Natural Habitat and Behavior of Deadly African Beasts*," said Lord Packenham, who had a thick volume balancing on his bony knees. "Says here that the crocodile drags its victim under water, and when the prey is large, it tucks it under a—"

"Enough!" Miss Kershaw shouted. "Can't you see how distressing this is to Nigel?! I mean Mr. Hargrave." She flashed her blue eyes in his direction.

Thankfully, Mr. Hargrave was spared any further remarks, as he was called away by the captain to discuss matters with officials over telegraph and radio.

Miss Kershaw, who had been following Mr. Hargrave's progress about the room, rose as though she meant to follow him, but then sat back down.

I wondered once again about how well the two knew each other.

"And I also find it very distressing. I don't think I will be able to sleep even a minute!" Mrs. Gladstone said, but no one was paying much attention to her.

"As a woman in touch with the spiritual world," Mr. Dalton said, "I would have thought you were not afraid of death."

"It's not death that I'm afraid of," Mrs. Gladstone countered and raised her chin. "It's the spirits I'm thinking of. A violent death like this creates unrest in the ether. Those spiritual beings are very sensitive. A lot of them have experienced violent deaths of their own. They will be keeping me up all night!"

"What do you mean?" Mrs. Babcock asked, frowning. I was surprised that a woman of science would encourage Mrs. Gladstone's fancies.

"The spirits will be very restless," replied Mrs. Gladstone, her black eyes darting about the room. "When there is a young spirit among them, they want to learn everything about the spirit's life here on earth and how the spirit died. They will be troubling me with questions all night and will not allow me to go to sleep."

Mrs. Gladstone's companion nodded in agreement, though with some reservation.

Mr. Dalton, who had grown increasingly impatient during Mrs. Gladstone's speech, got up from his chair abruptly. "Enough of this female foolishness! Don't you see that there are more pressing issues here? There is the question of the dig to consider."

At the mention of the dig, Mr. Kershaw stirred and looked up with interest. "What question?"

"I mean that Lord Chatfield was the one in charge of the dig at Luxor, and now the question of concessions might come up again."

"Surely, the concession will go to his brother," Miss Kershaw said.

Mr. Hargrave walked back in, just at that moment. A change had come over his demeanor. There was a steely determination that was missing from his person before.

Others must have noticed the change as well, because Mrs. Babcock said, "What's the matter, Mr. Hargrave?"

He shook himself, as though coming out of a dream. "What? No, nothing...I hadn't realized until now that I am my brother's heir..."

"How fortunes have changed with just one stroke," Miss Kershaw said, scarcely breathing out the statement, and cast a furtive look at Mr. Hargrave.

He looked at her, and I thought that something unspoken passed between them. But I might have imagined it because the look was gone in an instant.

Miss Parker also must have grasped what Lord Chatfield's death meant for Mr. Hargrave's fortunes, because she smiled prettily at him. Poor Alistair, I thought.

Even Mrs. Babcock stared at Mr. Hargrave as though seeing him in a different light. He had suddenly become quite the eligible bachelor.

"What did the authorities say?" asked Mr. Kershaw.

"They advised us to proceed to Luxor. As the captain said, there is not much we can do here," Mr. Hargrave answered. "A message has been sent to other boats, downriver, to keep a lookout for my brother's body."

Mr. Hargrave was called away again, and the females of the group looked longingly after him.

We sat in silence for a bit. The Lords were leaning over the volume of *Deadly African Beasts*, discussing hippopotamus habits in hushed tones.

"The curse!" Mrs. Gladstone cried suddenly and sat up in her chair. "It's the curse!" She looked around at the other passengers. "I felt a bad omen the moment I stepped on this boat." My uncle nodded appreciatively. "The newspapers talked about a curse connected to Lord Chatfield and what he was digging!" She grabbed the beads around her neck as though they were a rosary.

"There are no such things as curses," said Mr. Kershaw.

"Oh, yes, there are. How would you explain all of these deaths?" Mrs. Gladstone countered.

"Accidents," Mr. Kershaw replied.

I looked towards Mrs. Babcock. I had expected her to chime in on the discussion of curses. But she looked lost in her own thoughts.

"But all in the same family?" Mrs. Gladstone continued. "The newspapers said an uncle just died in England. And now Lord Chatfield. And no human was responsible for their deaths! It must be the work of evil spirits."

"Mrs. Gladstone," Mr. Kershaw began, "The high priests had several standard curses they put at the entrances of tombs to warn away the more superstitious of thieves. The ancient Egyptians believed words held magic power. The curse discovered at Lord Chatfield's dig was similar to the one found in the Tutankhamen tomb. Nothing special or unique."

"Are you referring to the curse that killed the Earl of Carnarvon two years ago?" Alistair said.

Mr. Kershaw nodded. "But that death was a coincidence," he added.

The exchange did nothing to calm Mrs. Gladstone down. "We need to have a seance and ask the spirits," she suggested.

"I don't think that's quite appropriate under the circumstances," Miss Kershaw said.

"I don't see why not," Mrs. Gladstone retorted. "A person who has nothing to fear should not fear a seance. And anyhow, you don't need to participate. Our seance would be just as successful even with only two or three participants." She looked at her companion, who nodded.

"I'd like to participate," Mrs. Babcock said suddenly.

"Mrs. Babcock!" Miss Kershaw protested. "Surely not! Such drivel!"

"I feel uneasy leaving Lord Chatfield here in the water." Mrs. Babcock spoke slowly, as if trying to comprehend her own change of mind. Some of the tendrils of her hair had come undone, I noticed. "What if Lord Chatfield's spirit wants to return to us? If there are such things as spirits," she added.

The room was silent, as though others were contemplating the possibility of Lord Chatfield's spirit visiting us.

Why would a woman of science want to participate in a seance? I wondered.

"And speaking to his spirit could absolve feelings of guilt some of us might have about his death," Mrs. Babcock continued. "Some of us might feel a moral responsibility for not stopping him from doing such a foolish thing."

"You should not blame yourself, my dear," Mrs. Gladstone leaned over and patted her on the hand.

"Plus, no one who has worked in Egypt for as long as I have," Mrs. Babcock pressed on, "can doubt that there are some mysteries that cannot be explained. Aren't we, archaeologists, just seekers of truth and knowledge from thousands of years ago?" She looked at the archaeologist in the room. "The ancient Egyptians themselves believed in magic and communicating with the dead. I feel uneasy leaving Lord Chatfield here without exploring all the possibilities. Sometimes there are mysteries greater than our understanding." She shifted in her seat, as though uncomfortable with reconciling her scientific training with these more esoteric musings.

"Are you speaking of the curse?" Miss Kershaw asked, unable to hide the surprise in her voice.

"Yes, but not just words written on tomb walls," Mrs. Babcock answered. "I'm speaking of evil thoughts towards another person that set the wheels of destiny in motion. Evil thoughts that influence the turn of events."

"Are you suggesting that someone here wished Lord Chatfield harm, and that's why he died?" Miss Kershaw asked, the incredulity in her voice increasing.

"There are many people here who desired what Lord Chatfield had," Mrs. Babcock said and cast her gaze about the room, pausing suggestively at Mr. Kershaw and then Mr. Dalton. "People who desired the dig, the treasure it contained, even his..." She stopped because at that moment Mr. Hargrave walked back in.

I had the feeling that Mrs. Babcock had stopped herself from saying something. What was Mrs. Babcock suggesting? Did she hold someone here responsible for Lord Chatfield's death?

It was easy to follow her train of thought. She had paused at Mr. Kershaw, who had made no secret of wanting the site for himself and hinting that the brothers had somehow taken it from him in an underhanded way. And then she had looked at Mr. Dalton, who had been quite unreserved in his declaration that he was after the treasure of the undiscovered temple.

What was she about to say when Mr. Hargrave had walked in? Did she blame him for Lord Chatfield's death? Was she suggesting that he'd had a hand in his brother's demise?

But how was that even possible?

CHAPTER 12

It was quite late at night when the seance started.

While I expected only the female passengers to attend the session, and then only some of them, in the end, almost all passengers turned up. Extra chairs needed to be brought in.

It appeared that the events of the evening had prevented most people from sleeping, and they all made their way to the salon.

Only the Royal Society's members sent their excuses, complaining of sharp stomach pains and saying that dinner had not agreed with them.

Though I did not believe in seances, I was curious to observe not only Mrs. Gladstone at work but also the reaction of those in attendance. What was Mrs. Babcock hoping to gain from the seance? And did Mrs. Gladstone really believe herself to be a medium? Or was she just a fraud of some sort?

I wondered vaguely what the wife of a New York financier was doing holding seances.

But then again, I had three aunts who were quite devoted to the art and science of spiritualism, so I quite understood the attraction of the exercise.

The boat crew, under Mrs. Gladstone's supervision, had set up the salon. Red shawls with beads and fringe were draped over all the electric lights. Several Egyptian statuettes on the table—a bronze Sphinx, some cats, an obelisk—gently reflected the softened light. The windows were closed, shutting out the refreshing breeze of the Nile, and lit candles were positioned about the perimeter of the room.

These small changes had transformed the room, and the atmosphere felt oppressive and mysterious. I once again wondered about Mrs. Gladstone's familiarity with mediums.

At the center of the room stood a round table, with chairs all the way around, positioned as though marking off the hours on a clock face. All other furniture was pushed to the side.

At the twelve o'clock position sat Mrs. Gladstone. On her left, at one o'clock, sat her companion, Miss Parker, followed by Mrs. Babcock and then Alistair. At four o'clock sat Miss Kershaw, smoking, her eyes glittering mischievously in the dim light. I took a seat next to her.

Uncle Albert, who had insisted on accompanying me to see the "wonderful woman" in action, sat on my other side. Mr. Dalton, Mr. Kershaw, and, most unexpectedly, James completed the circle. He winked at me when he caught my eye. I wondered what he was doing here.

I smiled at him and raised an eyebrow, but he just shrugged lightly. Perhaps he found Mrs. Gladstone's insistence on a seance, and Mrs. Babcock's suggestion of foul play by evil thoughts, as intriguing as I did.

James and I hadn't had the opportunity to spend as much time together as I had anticipated. Somehow, the small quarters of the boat still did not afford us the proximity and intimacy that we craved. He was busy most of the time with Lord Packenham, though what kind of correspondence one could be conducting on a boat in the middle of the Nile was a mystery to me. I suspected Lord Packenham of conspiring to keep us apart, yet I could not fathom how the old devil knew that there was anything between us.

My thoughts of James were interrupted by the entrance of Mr. Hargrave.

"Mr. Hargrave!" Mrs. Babcock exclaimed. "What are you doing here?"

"I could ask you the same thing," he retorted, his face pale despite its tan. "A woman of your standing, engaging in this charade..."

His eyes slid to Miss Kershaw, who stuck out her chin and puffed out some smoke, as though taunting him to rebuke her as well. The smoke lingered in the still air of the room, snaking among the tinted lights like a spirit.

I expected Mr. Hargrave to call Mrs. Babcock away, but instead, he motioned to one of the attendants to bring him a chair, and he slid in between Alistair and Miss Kershaw. We all shifted down the circle to accommodate him.

"Not the person I expected at a seance, Mr. Hargrave," Miss Kershaw said, turning to look at him. A mix of emotions played upon her face. Was it curiosity or sorrow?

"I want to see what is being said. Anything that can be said behind my back can be said to my face," he stated, casting an accusatory glance at Mr. Kershaw and Mr. Dalton sitting across the table from him.

"You there," Mrs. Gladstone called out to one of the attendants rather rudely, "go check if anyone else is coming."

The attendant came back after a few minutes and shook his head.

"We can begin," said Mrs. Gladstone, and straightened up in her seat. She had dressed in layers of black lace for the occasion and her black eyes sparkled strangely with the reflected candlelight.

"You're not using the Ouija board, Mrs. Gladstone?" Miss Kershaw asked.

"No respectable medium uses the Ouija board, Miss Kershaw," the older woman answered, and cast a disapproving glance at her. "Too easy to manipulate. Or so my medium tells me. My medium certainly never uses one. And in my experience," she said, drilling her eyes into Miss Kershaw, "the spirits are very sensitive to any negative energy. They will not show up if there are any doubters among you. You need to clear your mind and become receptive to the powers which we are still too primitive to understand."

Mrs. Gladstone's eyes traveled around the table, examining each of us. She must have judged us in possession of sufficient positive energy, because she said, "Now, we can begin. Hold hands to form an unbroken circle, the symbol of an open vessel, the vessel we will become to receive the communications from the beyond."

We all joined hands and stood in silence.

"Turn off the electric lights," Mrs. Gladstone commanded the attendant by the door. The only light now was the faint flicker of candles.

Mrs. Gladstone closed her eyes. "I call upon the spirits ever-present, on those from time forgotten, to come forward and communicate with us. We are all your humble servants. Is there someone there?"

Silence.

And then, the distinct sound of a knock. I instinctively looked at the attendant, but his hands were hanging by his sides and he was standing some distance away from any surface he could have knocked on.

I returned my gaze to Mrs. Gladstone.

"Are you my spirit guide, the slave girl Nalhum?"

A knock.

"Is there a spirit with you that wants to talk to us?" Mrs. Gladstone asked.

A knock.

"What is your message for us?"

All of a sudden, Mrs. Gladstone's head fell back and her companion, Miss Parker, screamed. A jolt went around the circle. Mrs. Babcock gasped.

"I have a message for those sitting in this room," Mrs. Gladstone said in a strange voice. Her voice was deep yet hollow. It sounded as though it didn't emanate from her. It echoed strangely around the room. "Do not despair," the voice continued. "Your friend, and brother, is in a better place."

Mrs. Gladstone paused for what felt like quite a long time. Just when I thought nothing more would come, the voice spoke again. "The ancients are walking your brother towards the light."

"Spirit, are you talking about Lord Chatfield?" Mrs. Babcock interrupted, breathless.

"The one who was known by that name in his earthly form is here. In the realm of spirits, there are no titles. Only the purity of one's soul matters."

"Tell us about Lord Chatfield's death," Mrs. Babcock said. "Does he hold anyone here responsible?"

"Dark thoughts are all around you," the voice said. "But the darkest of thoughts are concealed by the ones who loot offerings made to the spirits. Beware. Do not disturb the tomb. Bad things will happen. Everyone on this ship is cursed."

I looked around the table to gauge everyone's reaction to this statement. The expression on most people's faces was one of bemusement. Only Miss Parker's countenance betrayed some fear. And a curious look passed over Mrs. Babcock's face. I wondered if she was worried about the curse.

"Our newest brother knew not what he was doing in his human form," the voice continued. "He was led astray by greed. He should not have disturbed the dead and their offerings. The gods punished him for taking their gifts away. If you insist on going forward with your desecration, the gods will have their revenge yet. If you insist on going forward to Luxor and digging the tomb, you are all cursed. More deaths will come."

A new ripple passed across the joined hands.

Suddenly, with a gasp for air, Mrs. Gladstone's head came back upright. All eyes turned to her.

"What is it? What happened?" she said in her normal voice, though she sounded quite hoarse.

"You were in a trance, Mrs. Gladstone," Miss Parker said.

"Was I?! How wonderful!" Mrs. Gladstone exclaimed. She disengaged her hands and moved them to her bosom. "I hope I didn't summon my dear departed cat, Bonnie. Did Bonnie come across? I apologize. She meows a lot."

"It wasn't a cat, Mrs. Gladstone," her companion said.

"Then who?" Mrs. Gladstone looked around with a doltish aspect.

"It was death," Miss Kershaw deadpanned.

"Death!" squealed Mrs. Gladstone, rather convincingly, I thought. "What did it say?"

"That we are all cursed," Miss Kershaw answered.

"The curse!" Mrs. Gladstone exclaimed again. "I knew we were not safe. Oh, I feel so hot all of a sudden. I need air." She got up from her chair, disturbing the table and dashed out to the deck. The candles flickered in her wake.

A good ploy to avoid questions, I thought.

Miss Parker lingered, looking uncomfortable and avoiding our eyes, though Alistair attempted to catch her attention several times.

What was Mrs. Gladstone playing at? Why was she warning us to stay away from the tomb? And why was she predicting another death? My thoughts suddenly drifted to the Lords. Had someone poisoned them at dinner?

Mr. Hargrave stormed out angrily after Mrs. Gladstone. I wondered if he would seek her out for an explanation. Miss Kershaw followed shortly after.

Mr. Dalton guffawed. "You can't tell me that you believe any of this?" he said.

Most discounted the seance as nonsense. Only Miss Parker and Mrs. Babcock remained silent. The group then broke up.

After escorting Uncle Albert to his cabin, while he'd gushed profusely about Mrs. Gladstone's abilities, I walked back to mine. In the shadows at the other end of the deck, I thought I saw two figures. But the moonless night prevented me from observing them clearly.

I slipped into my cabin and wondered if evil thoughts and curses truly could influence the course of events?

CHAPTER 13

The previous day's events were the talk of breakfast the next morning. Somehow, word of the seance overshadowed Lord Chatfield's death. Those who had not attended the performance were rather excited by the proclamation of another death to follow.

Mr. Dalton still declared the whole thing ridiculous, while Mrs. Babcock remained less categorical in her views.

I knew for a fact that there were no ghosts and spirits. And even if there were, I didn't believe in the power of self-purported mediums to contact them. My aunts' interest in the practice meant that I was quite familiar with the devices mediums, psychics, and clairvoyants employed to trick their audience.

By my estimation, Mrs. Gladstone had done quite well.

What intrigued me most about the previous night's performance, however, was that although Mrs. Gladstone professed herself an amateur, she'd proven to be quite an accomplished actress.

As seances went, it had been a tame one—no lights, no apparitions, no ectoplasm—yet the noises and knocks she'd produced were quite convincing. If she only dabbled in spiritualism, as she continuously asserted, then why was she so knowledgeable about the tricks of the trade, as it were?

But I kept my thoughts on the matter private.

I noted that Mrs. Gladstone had not made an appearance at breakfast. Was she perhaps avoiding Mr. Hargrave, or was she avoiding being asked more questions about her prediction from the previous night?

Mr. Hargrave sat with his back to us, and I wondered if he regarded the seance as a mockery of his brother's memory. Perhaps it was, and now I was sorry I had taken part in it.

The strained atmosphere prevailing under the canopy of the sun deck, where breakfast was served, was quite at odds with the beautiful morning. The air was still fresh, and the sun sparkled playfully on the waters of the Nile. In the distance, downriver from us, the full sails of a graceful white dahabiya were visible.

The dahabiya seemed to be gaining on us, and an exchange of shouts between our crew and the crew of the sailboat caught the breakfast attendees' attention.

The more geographically challenged among our group wondered aloud if the boat was from

Cairo, carrying British officials sent to deal with the Lord Chatfield complication. But I knew it was impossible for a sailboat leaving Cairo yesterday evening to catch up with us this morning.

That fact made the approaching boat no less interesting. We had passed many boats on the river, but apart from the occasional shouted greeting, none of the vessels had made such an effort to engage with us.

We watched as the captain of the dahabiya spoke excitedly for a few minutes with our own captain.

Captain Saleeb then ascended the stairs to the sun deck. All assembled followed his progress through the breakfast tables with scrutiny.

"Lady Caroline," he said, pausing at my table, "the captain of the *Al'amal* says that there is a person on board who is a friend of yours and wishes to speak with you."

"Really?" I said, perplexed. I was quite certain that I did not know anyone currently visiting Egypt. "I wonder who it could be? I don't know anyone in Egypt."

Wilford, who had been helping Uncle Albert deal with a particularly troublesome date fruit, stepped forward. "If you permit me, My Lady. A few possibilities spring to mind."

I nodded.

"Roger Pinckle, of the British-Egyptian Cotton Company, is a distant cousin. There is also the prospect that it could be your other distant cousin, Josiah Flounder, the famed missionary, explorer, and writer. He and his wife Ester, a noted composer of hymns in the local vernacular, are known for their preference of vacationing in Egypt after the rigors of spreading the good word along the shores of the Kasai river. However, it is also entirely likely to be—"

"Thank you Wilford," I said. None of these possibilities promoted any excitement in me. And why would these people want to speak with me rather than Uncle Albert? "Perhaps it's easiest if I were to investigate directly," I concluded and let our captain lead me on.

A woman stood on the deck of the dahabiya, wearing a rather fetching *eau de Nil* suit of Parisian provenance. She looked vaguely familiar, and I wondered if it could indeed be cousin Ester —though the Parisian couture disallowed that theory—but her face was hidden by a voluminous sun hat.

"Ahoy there, Gassy!" the woman's voice bellowed across the water with the power of Great George ringing from the south tower of Liverpool Cathedral.

"Poppy!" I exclaimed, recognizing my chum Persephone Kettering-Thrapston. Or *Lady Ottley*, as was her new courtesy title.

"I snagged the last sailboat!" she yelled back. "Though the proper sailing skills seem to be lost on these men." She cast a disparaging look at the crew, who shrunk back from her gaze. "The captain was quite adamant that the top speed of his boat is 8 knots. I showed him that with the correct approach, a speed of 14 knots is quite possible."

I mused that Poppy had quite missed the point of the leisurely and relaxing voyage a dahabiya offered. "What are you doing here? Is everything alright?" I said anxiously.

"Yes, everything is fine!" Poppy replied. "Never been better!"

"Has something happened to Leopold?" I asked.

Poppy had lately married James' older brother Leopold, Viscount Ottley, and the heir apparent to the Earl of Haswell. Poppy and Leopold had undertaken a whirlwind romance, though, to be frank, Leopold had mostly appeared windswept in the force of Poppy's gale. However, as Leopold held the dubious distinction among London bookmakers as the bachelor with the longest odds in a generation, the match had been quite fortuitous for him.

And while the honeymoon had been delayed because Poppy's father had bought the happy couple an estate as a wedding gift, and Poppy had insisted on having it immediately remodeled, I quite expected her to be on a honeymoon trip somewhere in Europe by now. Not seeing Leopold on board, I worried that Poppy had dispatched him to attend their honeymoon on his own for some reason.

"No, why? Leo is right here," she said, using her husband's pet name, and gestured towards the cabin. "Though he is recovering from a bit of seasickness, poor lamb," she added in a tender tone.

"Then why are you not on your honeymoon?" I demanded.

"Well, Leo had his heart set on Paris. But I cannot fathom why everyone considers Paris so romantic. One can pop over at any time to visit the couture houses and restaurants. One tires of tulle and truffles so."

Poppy was indeed a treasured customer of the Parisian couture houses. And of the city's restaurants, if one had to be entirely candid.

"Plus, I couldn't see how a trip to Paris would advance Leo's interests in life," she continued. "One needs something more bracing on one's honeymoon, don't you think? I considered Kenya for a spot of shooting. But as Leo would rather look at animals through his binoculars than through the crosshairs of a rifle,"—she rolled her eyes—"I decided that a jaunt up the Nile would not go amiss."

Perhaps because he'd heard his name mentioned, Leopold emerged from the cabin to join Poppy. He waved weakly.

Only when one had the opportunity to observe the happy couple side by side, did the incongruity of their match strike the observer fully.

Poppy was the type of girl the British Beef Co. made marrow stock for, and the Egyptian sun had added a healthy glow to her skin. Next to her, Leopold seemed slight and sickly. I could see that the Egyptian heat was not agreeing with him. Beads of perspiration littered his balding crown while the pleasant breeze carelessly disarranged his carefully combed hair.

"Now, down to business," Poppy continued. "I have been driving the captain quite hard to catch up with you." I looked past Poppy to the man in the traditional jalabiya cowering in her shadow. I might have been mistaken, but he seemed to be sending me pleading looks.

"Why?" I asked, intrigued.

"If you must know, I'm angling for Leo to secure a spot on the Royal Society by the end of next year. So when I heard the members were heading to Egypt, I just knew we had to join you. What is the assignment this time?"

"It's beetles!" I yelled across the water.

"Excellent!" Poppy turned to Leopold and patted him heartily on the back, making him stagger. "Tell me, is the Golden Platypus still the top prize?"

"No, it's a mummified cat," I answered.

"Pity. I just had the drawing room remodeled in golden tones to match the prize. I suppose I'll need to cable the designers that an Egyptian theme is in order." Poppy cast a warning look at Leopold, giving him to understand that she expected him to do nothing less than to bring the prized cat home.

Leopold swallowed audibly.

"Where are you headed to next?" Poppy asked.

"Luxor," I said.

"We'll see you there!" She signed off with an ebullient wave and proceeded to escort Leo to a canvas lounger under a thick canopy.

But then, as though just remembering something, she turned around. "I say, I didn't expect to catch up with you quite so soon. By my calculations, even with the improved sailing practices, we've reached you a day or two too early." Concern darkened her face. "Is it producing sufficient steam?" Poppy asked while casting a critical glance at the funnel of our steamboat. "Do you need me to come on board and organize your crew?"

Captain Saleeb flinched next to me. No doubt the captain of the *Al'amal* had wasted no opportunity to bring him up to speed on Poppy's temperament.

"There is nothing wrong with the boat, Poppy," I answered. "But we've had a delay due to a bit of misadventure."

"I say!" Poppy exclaimed. "You do get in the most frightful scrapes, Caroline!"

"It's not murder," I said rather testily. "This time," I added. "One of our passengers, Lord

Chatfield, was attacked by a crocodile yesterday evening."

"Is he alright?" Poppy asked.

"Doesn't appear so. He's nowhere to be found. So we can only assume that the crocodile took him under water..." I did not elaborate.

"I say! Rotten luck!"

"Quite," I replied. "Captain Saleeb tells us that crocodiles usually don't attack humans. We are too big for them to eat. Lord Chatfield must have disturbed a nest or something like that. Poor man."

I wanted to tell her about the seance, and the rest of the passengers, but as our conversation was impossible not to overhear, I decided to put it aside for another time.

But as the cause of our delay was not technical, Poppy seemed to have lost interest in the topic. "Off to Luxor we go! To find a beetle! We'll need to put in a few trial runs!" She clipped Leopold on the back again, which this time made him cough. "Oh, and Caroline," she shouted to me as her sailboat pulled away, "I expect you for drinks on board at Luxor, first thing. And James!"

And with that, Poppy turned around and set about giving instructions to the hapless crew, who scattered around the boat, and began pulling various ropes and sails.

I watched the elegant dahabiya glide smoothly on the river for a while, until I could see it no longer. I longed to be on that boat, in Poppy's company—so confident and carefree. Instead, I was consigned to a boat full of secrets, suspicion, and death.

CHAPTER 14

Seeing Poppy made me think longingly of the world beyond the boat, and I began to feel like a prisoner just before release. While the end was in sight, the prospect of still more days on water, in the confines of the same society, left me restless and irritable. Our trek up the river now seemed laborious and slow, and the landscape—monotonous.

I feared I would make a break for it and jump into the murky waters before we reached Luxor.

At least the inane ramblings of the Royal Society had ceased.

A trend that had started the night of the seance, continued into the following days. And while my opinion of Mrs. Gladstone hadn't changed, and I still suspected her of being a fraud, her prophecy seemed to come to pass. One by one, the Lords of the Royal Society took turns complaining of stomach ailments, became confined to their rooms, and then to their beds.

Under normal circumstances, I would not have worried. The Lords were known to have delicate digestions, and a venture into a foreign land, faced with unfamiliar food—so soon after the infamous internal battle with the Japanese fish, which had landed the members in a sanatorium—was perhaps unwise.

Yet, with Mrs. Gladstone's pronouncement of more deaths to come fresh in my mind, I began to worry that one of the Lords would be next to go.

I endeavored to lift my mood by reflecting that if the Lords of the Royal Society had not been confined to their cabins, they would certainly be placing wagers on the soul most likely to fulfill Mrs. Gladstone's prediction. (I suspected the private secretaries had stepped in to fill that void, but they did not include me in their diversions).

But as things stood, the Lords' maladies were not a laughing matter, and I soon began to suspect that someone was slowly poisoning them.

It had transpired that the ship was not well equipped to handle the noble afflictions of the Royal Society, and it had been Mrs. Babcock who had produced a bottle of home-made remedy. A veteran of Egypt, she knew just how to treat stomach discomfort.

Returning from visiting the sick, where she had administered the vile concoction swirling in her brown bottle to the latest victim, Mrs. Babcock echoed my dark thoughts: "It is difficult to determine whether one is being poisoned in Egypt." She let out a nervous chuckle.

I perked up. "Do you think the Lords are being poisoned?" I asked. I wondered what had prompted her remark.

"Oh, no. No such thing!" She looked about her, alarmed. "Forgive me. It was just my attempt at a joke. One doesn't mean to insult the local food, but I must say that one is not likely to meet with so many digestive complaints on a trip up the Thames."

Her statement was met with endorsement around the lounge and conversation drifted towards tales of hardship in foreign lands. As so many of the passengers were so well-traveled, only Mrs. Gladstone, lately returned to our society, and her companion, could not contribute a tale of woe.

I turned my attention to Mrs. Gladstone, revisiting thoughts that had troubled me over the past few days. What had been her objective during the seance? Had she really felt some evil power at work? And why had she been so quick to predict another death?

Had Mrs. Gladstone seen something suspicious? Had she observed one of the passengers doing something wrong? Was the seance her attempt at warning the perpetrator that she was on to them? But such an act would be foolish. And though Mrs. Gladstone had all the appearances of a fool, her sharp eyes gave her true persona away.

Was she an attention seeker? Did she simply

like causing discord? Or was her seance the prelude to something entirely more nefarious? In short, was she setting the stage for murder? And if that were so, was the next victim one of the Lords, or was she worried that someone was out to murder her?

Yet, who did Mrs. Gladstone know on the boat that would want her dead? By all indications, she had never left America, and only knew Miss Parker, her companion. And although Mr. Dalton was American, and found Mrs. Gladstone irritating, and Miss Kershaw had gone to university in New York, neither appeared to want to do the older woman any lasting harm.

Thinking of Miss Kershaw reminded me of a thought I'd had on a couple of previous occasions. She was in the habit of exchanging glances with Mr. Hargrave. Just how well did they know each other? It almost seemed inconceivable that they did not know each other better than it appeared. One would think that being of a similar age and sharing an interest in Egyptology, their paths would have crossed both professionally and socially while in Egypt.

Then again, perhaps the time Miss Kershaw had spent in New York had been time enough to sever any passing acquaintance. Plus, Mr. Kershaw's dislike of Mr. Hargrave was evident. Perhaps the young woman, even if she liked Mr. Hargrave, kept her distance on her father's account.

My thoughts then turned to Alistair. Nothing had materialized on that front. While courteous, Miss Parker did not pay him more attention than she did to any other man on the boat. But there was still hope. The Egyptian season was well known for facilitating marriage proposals, and young women departed the country with several offers in hand.

The notion of marriage proposals turned my thoughts to James. With Lord Packenham confined to a sick bed, James was required to sit by his side, taking incessant notes on the terms of his lordship's ever-changing will and testament.

Thus, my days till Luxor were chiefly occupied by Uncle Albert—who somehow had avoided being poisoned—bumbling about with beetles. Unperturbed by the events of the past few days, he neither mentioned Lord Chatfield, nor commented on Mrs. Gladstone's prediction. Breakfasts usually caught him unawares with an outsized magnifying glass, examining a not entirely dead specimen from one of his overnight nets. Each time the creature strove to crawl away, Uncle prodded it gently back to its position under his hand lens. These daily tests of wits between beetle and man were much to the distaste of Mrs. Babcock, who huffed in the direction of our table at regular intervals.

The morning of our arrival in Luxor dawned clear and bright, and the prospect of stepping on dry land had transformed the atmosphere on the boat.

While relations between Mr. Hargrave and Mrs. Gladstone were still strained, she had refrained from making any more fatalistic pronouncements, and the two were almost civil to each other. Mrs. Babcock's concoction had also worked wonders, and the Lords were up and about, getting into everyone's way, checking their air nets for any final haul. The matter of the prophesied death seemed to have been forgotten.

The mood had lifted to such an extent that Mr. Hargrave renewed his invitation to the Royal Society for a visit to his dig. One thing led to another, and the visit turned to a call for dinner at the dig, and then to an invitation to spend the night at the camp, like archeologists, in field tents. In its final reiteration, since we were already to sleep in tents, the invitation also included a rare stint at excavating the tomb.

Mr. Hargrave assured us that the tomb was sufficiently big to require all the help he could get.

"Most of the work is unskilled, mainly hauling sand out of the tomb, so anyone could do it," Mrs. Babcock clarified, with the Lords uncertain how to receive the statement.

With his brother gone, Mr. Hargrave also conceded that he would have to take on more of an administrative role, so Mr. Kershaw and his daughter were invited to become part of the archeological team. Mr. Kershaw looked dubious about the honor, but his daughter accepted on his behalf.

And after a quick word from Mrs. Babcock, suggesting in measured tones that extending the invitation for a visit and dinner to only some of the passengers could be considered rude, Mr. Hargrave added even Mr. Dalton, Mrs. Gladstone, and her companion to the list.

I wondered vaguely why a woman who had warned us of the perils of going to Mr. Hargrave's tomb, and had foretold death to those who visited the site, would be interested in joining us. But Mrs. Gladstone was nothing if not an enigma.

With entertainment thus ensured, the Lords of the Royal Society turned their attention to Alistair. In addition to the boat passage, Alistair had been tasked with securing a hotel.

Hope of decent accommodations was low among the Lords and it sank even lower as Alistair, scarlet-faced, distributed hotel vouchers to each.

"I say!" the Lords of the Royal Society cried, staring at the pieces of paper in their hands with befuddled expressions. "What is the meaning of this?" They waved the papers about.

It fell upon their private secretaries to explain the intricacies of using coupons for hotels—the bearers exchanged the vouchers for a stay at one of Cook and Son's purpose-built hotels along the Nile.

Most Lords took in the news wearing a

countenance that suggested they were not positive this had been worth leaving their sick bed for.

But duty was stronger than any temporal discomfort. "Stiff upper lip!" the veterans of empire-building cried, and set forth to examine their lodgings. They were determined to rebuild their strength for the trials of the coming days—namely, the hunt for dung beetles—and recuperate the losses of specimens sustained during their convalescence.

But before we could disembark and examine our living quarters, our boat was met at the Luxor landing by a representative of the British government.

He introduced himself as Mr. Lowell and gathered us in the boat's dining room, despite the groans from those familiar with the protracted rituals favored by British bureaucrats.

CHAPTER 15

Mr. Lowell, however, appeared to be not quite the typical British civil servant.

He had a rugged handsomeness, which, in my experience, came only from a hearty balance of sport and fun. His wide shoulders, healthy tan, thick sandy hair, and perfect teeth, all suggested a preference for the great outdoors, and speculative adventure, over desks. No doubt, being stationed in Egypt put him at an advantage over his colleagues in London.

One could easily muse for hours about what transgression had dispatched him to this relatively quiet corner of the globe. Why was he not in London turning the heads of debutants? Or was he one of those young men one hears about clandestinely, who travel the globe on secret missions for the government? What was hidden among the sands of Egypt that solicited his presence here? Surely, he was not in Luxor for its profusion of dung beetles.

Had I not had an unofficial understanding with James, and been quite madly in love with him, Mr. Lowell would have been a rather dashing young man to spend a few days with, getting to know the ruins of Luxor.

I pulled myself back to the present, located James by Lord Packenham's side, and smiled at him. Mr. Lowell's arrival, whether due to his charm or the prospect of some protracted official procedures related to Lord Chatfield's death, had created quite a buzz among the passengers. Even James observed him with something akin to bemusement playing across his face.

But proceedings turned out to be less interesting than Mr. Lowell's presence on the boat had promised, and after a series of questions ascertaining the facts surrounding Lord Chatfield's death, the matter was concluded. Mr. Hargrave was invited to visit Mr. Lowell's office to contact his lawyers in London and to begin the paperwork necessary to inherit his brother's title and estate.

And with that, we descended upon The Winter Palace hotel like a bunch of scurrying beetles.

The Winter Palace proved to be quite a triumph on Alistair's part. Either he, or more likely the agent in London, had booked what had to be the nicest hotel in Egypt. Situated on the waterfront, it was just a short donkey ride to the temple of Luxor, as the concierge informed us.

It rivaled any in Europe for position, view, and proximity to sites. Coupled with its opulent interior, one would be hard-pressed to find such an agreeable hotel, even in Venice.

The hotel was well known to newspaper readers around the world as the center where Mr. Carter, after opening the Tutankhamen tomb three years ago, had begun leaving messages on its bulletin board about his progress. It was also the place where the world press congregated in order to gather information and file reports contrived to feed the world's insatiable fascination with Egyptomania. And though some of the excitement had died down, the hotel was still quite crowded and overrun by journalists and adventurers. Lord Chatfield's absence from our boat had not gone unnoticed, and we were accosted in the lobby by men in fedoras.

Once in my room, I threw the windows open and stepped onto my little balcony.

The warm, dry wind washed over me as I marveled at the sights. Before me was the Nile, so close, I could almost reach out and touch it. I scanned the moorings along the river, but could not see Poppy's sailboat yet. To the right stood the grand temples of Luxor, and beyond that, down the Avenue of the Sphinxes, were the golden-hued temples at Karnak—which I had spied from the boat on our approach to Luxor—with their awe-inspiring columns. Across the river, on the west bank, in the distant desert hills, was the Valley of the Kings, and the famed Tutankhamen tomb. That general direction was also the location of Mr.

Hargrave's dig, the tomb of Ahmose, as far as I had understood.

Luxor exuded an atmosphere quite different to Cairo—it lacked the traffic, the noise, and the humidity. It felt like a garden of archaeological delights. The clangs of metal against rock and the cries of workers at the various digs across the river carried on the breeze. Numerous black holes, indicating opened tombs, dotted the rocky outcrops on the west bank.

This was the Egypt I had imagined when I had started on this trip, in all its majesty and mystery.

After the closed quarters of the boat, I relished my freedom. I lingered in my room, luxuriated in a long bath, took lunch in the sanctuary of my quarters, and in the early afternoon began getting ready for our excursion to Mr. Hargrave's site. I was quite excited by the prospect of staying at an ancient Egyptian archeological dig after dark.

Our little group—minus Mr. Hargrave and Mrs. Babcock, who were already at the site—gathered in front of the hotel, just as the sun was going down. Luxor's sights radiated in the late afternoon, their golden glow contrasting beautifully against the blue and purple hues of the endless sky behind them.

Porters had taken our overnight bags, and all we had to do was cross the river on a ferry to the other bank.

"All the tombs are located on the other side

of the river," Lord Fetherly was saying, consulting the guidebook in his hands while we were riding the ferry. "Says here that the temples and tombs we see along the west bank are those of Theban Necropolis. Further in are the tombs of the queens and then the kings."

"Where is Mr. Hargrave's dig located?" Mrs. Gladstone asked.

Mr. Kershaw's explanation served more to confuse than enlighten us as to its precise location.

But we need not have worried. The hotel's concierge had arranged all the details of our excursion and upon disembarking, donkeys were waiting to convey us to the site.

Having already had some practice with donkeys at Memphis, then Giza, and then a third run at Beni Hasan, the ride to the tomb of Ahmose went almost without a hitch. Except for Lord Mantelbury losing his seat a few times, and having to be carried up a hill, we were making good progress.

The path wound through a valley surrounded by cliffs pockmarked by opened tombs. Then the road straightened, and we rode through a narrow opening between two hills, which stood as a pair of sentinels overlooking the road. By this time, twilight had descended over the valley, and the rock faces around us were thrown into darkness.

As we crossed the threshold of the two hills, a beautiful clearing opened up in front of us, protected on all sides by cliffs. Candles, their flames calm in the still evening air, lined our path to a tent that glowed softly from within. We had arrived at Mr. Hargrave's dig.

The sparse, camp-like furnishings of the dinner tent did not detract from the sublime feeling of eating dinner at a real ancient Egyptian site. Everyone was properly subdued by the occasion and the conversation was quite civil, centering around the organization and operation of the dig.

"The death of my brother has had quite a dampening effect on the local workers," Mr. Hargrave was saying. "They think his death is a warning. The foreman said he's had a difficult time persuading them to continue looking for the temple and the treasure."

"The locals have no such qualms when it comes to raiding tombs for their own benefit," Mrs. Babcock said, sounding quite indignant. "They are superstitious only when there is an Englishman paying them, demanding higher pay for working on a cursed tomb."

"Indeed!" one of the Lords of the Royal Society piped up. "Reminds me of my time in India." And conversation turned to weighing up India against Egypt.

My own thoughts drifted to the curse. Though Lord Chatfield's death was never far from my thoughts, I had all but forgotten about the curse attached to this tomb. I stole a quick glance at Mrs.

Gladstone and wondered if she would bring up her prediction again.

But when Mrs. Gladstone spoke, it was on a quite different matter. "Are you going to show us the mummy while we are here?" she asked in her prosaic manner. Her dark eyes glinted.

Mr. Hargrave glared at the woman for a few moments.

"I believe you are in luck, Mrs. Gladstone," Mrs. Babcock said, jumping in. "The mummy is currently out of its sarcophagus, ready to be photographed."

An enthusiastic murmur passed around the table at the prospect of seeing a mummy *in situ*.

"Mr. Hargrave," I turned to our gracious host, "what are we to expect of our adventure of staying at the site overnight?" I was quite elated by the undertaking of sleeping in the desert, among the tombs of ancient Egypt, and could not wait to go to bed.

"It does get quite cold," Mr. Hargrave said. "As we are in the desert, the temperatures drop drastically overnight."

"And you might hear some strange noises," Mrs. Babcock added.

"What strange noises?" Mrs. Gladstone asked. "The dead coming to life?!"

Mr. Kershaw laughed. "Watch out for that mummy out of its sarcophagus!"

"Mr. Kershaw, please," Mrs. Babcock objected. "Sometimes wild animals wander into the camps —jackals, foxes, hyenas. Other times it's tomb robbers." She sent a condescending glance at Mr. Dalton.

A flicker of amusement danced in Mr. Dalton's eyes before he replied. "I've heard that there is nothing much of value here, despite all this talk of curse and treasure."

"There will be no tomb robbers," Mr. Hargrave interjected. "There are enough local guards stationed around the site. We'll be safe from animals and thieves."

By the end of dinner, the Lords of the Royal Society, citing rheumatism, psoriasis, nephrolithiasis, ulcerative colitis, and insomnia, had all declared that they would be riding back to the comforts of the hotel—perhaps motivated by the talk of animals and robbers—but promised to join us again in the morning for the viewing of the mummy. The decision was not well received by the Society's private secretaries, and they trudged reluctantly after their employers, casting longing glances back. I smiled at James when he looked at me questioningly and shrugged my shoulders. As I was my uncle's niece before I was his secretary, the rules did not apply to me. I was staying overnight at the camp.

I noticed Mrs. Gladstone hesitating about whether to leave with the Royal Society, but in the end she decided to remain, mentioning something about communing with ancient spirits.

Those of us lucky enough to spend the night at the dig—Mr. and Miss Kershaw, Mrs. Gladstone and her assistant, Mr. Dalton, and myself—were shown to our sleeping quarters.

Each of us was to sleep in their own tent, equipped with a camp bed and little else. I quite looked forward to the experience. The austerity of the camp reminded me of my days at the Boughton Monchelsea School for Girls, though the camp was equipped with better sanitary facilities.

As I lay in my bed, separated from the elements by only the canvas of my tent, I listened out for the noises Mrs. Babcock had promised us. I heard the coughs of my companions and the squeak of springs as they shifted in their beds. But as people began to fall asleep, a stillness overtook the camp. I now heard the distant calls of nocturnal animals, a fox bark, a howl, the soft whisper of sands shifting, perhaps a rodent, and from time to time the eerie whistles of gusts of wind passing through crevices in rocks. I wondered if I would ever get to sleep.

I awoke to a strange noise coming quite close from without my tent. A shadow played upon the canvas, but it was gone within a moment.

Robbers! I jumped out of bed.

CHAPTER 16

I threw the flaps of my tent open, but dared not go any further. If the camp really was invaded by tomb robbers, perhaps staying inside the tent and letting the guards deal with them was more prudent.

Though the shadow was now gone, the singular noise I had heard accompanying it, like a deep and painful moan, remained in my ears.

I strained to detect any scuffle in the distance. Were the guards on alert? Had they apprehended the criminals? But it sounded as though only our small group had been awoken by the disturbance. I could hear people stirring about quite close.

It was difficult to see anything. The darkness was utterly impenetrable, broken only by torches near each of the tents, which did little more than throw a small pool of light on the ground. In the distance, the glow of the fire in the middle of the camp, lit to keep animals away, was visible.

"Did you hear that?" Mrs. Gladstone's voice asked out of the darkness.

"And saw it," I said, trying to make out her

shape. Now a light from a torch was moving around the tents.

"You did?!" Mrs. Gladstone asked, her voice quite shrill. "What was it?"

"I don't know. I can't be positive. I saw its shadow across the canvas of my tent. It must have been carrying a torch. It had a human shape, I think. Or at least it had something that looked like a head. But it was quite tall. Perhaps someone is playing a prank on us. Perhaps Mr. Kershaw," I suggested, thinking back to the conversation during dinner. Though the prankster could have been Mr. Dalton as well, I conceded.

"But that voice," Mrs. Gladstone protested. "It was like a voice from the beyond. Miss Parker, Daisy, I feel very cold. Evil spirits are among us."

For a moment I wondered if it had been Mrs. Gladstone who had made the voice.

"Over here!" Mr. Dalton called out.

Suddenly we were joined by Mr. Hargrave and Mrs. Babcock, both carrying electric torches.

"Follow me," Mr. Hargrave said.

We hurried towards Mr. Dalton's voice in the direction of the fire pit.

"What is it, man?" Mr. Hargrave cried out when the figure of Mr. Dalton came into view. He had his own torch, which was illuminating his face in a quite ghostly way. "What is the commotion about?" Mr. Hargrave asked again as we came to the fire.

Mr. Dalton did not answer, but turned his torch to a figure next to him.

Sitting near the fire, reclining on a safari chair, was a person wearing what looked like a tattered linen suit. Even with the light from the fire, it was difficult to make the person out.

Only, looking at him more closely, there was something strange about this person. He wasn't sitting on the chair. He was leaning on top of it in the most unnatural way. And he wasn't moving. He looked quite rigid. The proclamation Mrs. Gladstone had made a few days ago burst into my mind.

"Is it a body?" I asked, squinting into the darkness.

"Oh, most definitely," Mr. Dalton answered, but there was a note that was not quite right in his voice. Was Mr. Dalton smiling?

We had stopped instinctively when we had spotted Mr. Dalton and the mysterious person. But now we advanced towards them. And then I saw it. It was a mummy.

Mrs. Gladstone, or perhaps Miss Parker, screamed.

"It's only a mummy," said Miss Kershaw, standing by her father's side. I had not noticed when the Kershaws had joined us.

But I was inclined to agree with Mrs. Gladstone's view of the situation. The mummy stood there, leaning stiffly against the chair.

Loose bandages, darkened in places with age or embalming resin, dangled from its body. The black head, its bandages peeled away, stood out against the white body. The embers of the dying fire illuminated its features—a grotesque mask of dry, crumbling layers which had shriveled as the tissue and muscles underneath had rotted away. The empty eyes stared unseeing into the fire.

But the most astonishing feature of the mummy had to be its hat. It wore an archeologist's pith helmet.

I shivered and wrapped my arms around myself.

"That's Lord Chatfield's chair," said Mrs. Babcock, sounding alarmed. "I recognize it. It's the leather one, not canvas like all the others. It's from his tent. And is that Lord Chatfield's pith helmet?"

"Don't be silly, woman," cried Mr. Kershaw. "We all saw him go down with it. Egypt is awash with pith helmets. It could be anyone's."

"He did have two," Mr. Hargrave said.

"Then someone should check if this is his," Mr. Dalton suggested.

"I'll go check his tent," said Mrs. Babcock.

"My brother was very particular about his possessions and losing them. If this is his, it will have his initials stamped on the leather headband on the inside," Mr. Hargrave said, and reached for the hat. "By Jove, there is a note pinned to the mummy!"

"What is it?" Mr. Dalton asked and leaned down to see. I wondered why he hadn't spotted it himself.

"It's written in hieroglyphics," Mr. Hargrave said. "Let me see. It will take me a moment to decipher it." He shone his torch on the note.

"Bring it to the light here," Mr. Kershaw suggested and waved his more powerful lantern. "We can look at it together. Margaret is very good at hieroglyphics."

The archeologists—Miss Kershaw and her father, Mr. Hargrave, and even Mr. Dalton—gathered around the note. Mr. Kershaw was holding up the lantern to illuminate the message.

Mrs. Gladstone, Miss Parker, and I moved closer together. Whether it was to feel warmer or safer, I could not say. I looked about for the guards, but they were nowhere to be seen.

"The hat is not in his tent," announced Mrs. Babcock as she made her way back to us. "What is it?" she asked upon seeing the group of experts gathered in the darkness around the lantern.

"A note, in hieroglyphics, was attached to the mummy'," I said.

"Oh! I've never been very good with hieroglyphs," she said to me and went to join the circle of archeologists.

"It's a warning," said Mr. Kershaw. "You see the *amenta* symbol here? The sign of the underworld. And the *feather of Maat* here, representing justice."

"Yes, yes," said Mr. Dalton rather testily. "But what is the full message?"

"It's a warning to keep out of the tomb of Ahmose," announced Miss Kershaw. "It foretells more deaths." She looked around at all gathered. "Someone is trying to scare us away from exploring it." She cast a quick glance at Mrs. Gladstone, who caught her breath. "I wonder why?" Miss Kershaw added, and exchanged a brief look with Mr. Hargrave, who had been watching her quite closely as she spoke.

I speculated about how many of the others suspected Mrs. Gladstone as the mummy culprit.

"It's a standard message," countered Mr. Kershaw, "written on many tombs. It was reprinted in the London newspapers after the discovery of the Tutankhamen tomb. And I think the Cook and Son travel guide also has a copy of it."

"It's the curse," Mrs. Gladstone whispered. "It's the curse, come to get us."

"Enough about this curse," said Miss Kershaw. "This is clearly a prank, played by a human. A human that is here, in this camp. No mummy can move itself."

"Do you think it was the same person who made the strange noise?" Mrs. Gladstone asked.

"Obviously," I said. "Whoever did this wanted us to wake up and find the mummy."

After a while, the local guards, who had managed to sleep through the whole ordeal, and did not awake until Mr. Hargrave roused them, came to take the mummy away. They seemed agitated and reluctant to go near it. Miss Kershaw translated that they believed the spirit of Lord Chatfield had come to warn them about the tomb, that the mummy was a warning from the dead Lord Chatfield to abandon this site.

I lay awake for a long while after the mummy was carried away by the guards.

Was this a trick played by the local workers to strengthen their case and the claim that the tomb was cursed and haunted, thus demanding a higher payment for their work? Yet they seemed genuinely surprised to find the mummy by the fire pit, and quite upset that it had somehow made its way out of the tent where they had left it for photography.

Or was this instead a deception invented by Mrs. Gladstone to reinforce her prophecy? More than one person had looked at her suspiciously, though no one had accused her out loud. But why was Mrs. Gladstone so insistent that another death was to come? What did she have to gain from it?

Or perhaps this was a prank carried out by someone who had a vested interest in stopping Mr. Hargrave from continuing his work at this site. Was it Mr. Kershaw, who wanted the dig to himself? Was he sabotaging Mr. Hargrave's work here? Was he trying to erode the confidence of the locals in Mr. Hargrave's authority over the dig?

What about Mr. Dalton? If the dig stopped, the area would become more accessible to the local tomb robbers with whom he was perhaps in league. I had no doubt that he bought many of his antiques from the more unscrupulous locals, who did not think to register their finds with the Department of Antiquities.

Whoever it was, the mummy provided some clues to the prankster's identity.

First, the person must have known where to find the mummy. Second, the chair and the hat —the perpetrator must have known the location of Lord Chatfield's tent, and his personal items. But then again, that could have been anyone of our party. Lord Chatfield's tent was obviously the biggest and the most centrally located tent in the camp. It would have been easy for any of us to sneak into Lord Chatfield's tent and pinch a few of his personal items to make us think that his spirit had come back to warn us about the tomb's curse.

But the third clue, the hieroglyphic message, was even more telling. There were only a handful of people in our group who possessed the skill to write in hieroglyphs—Mr. Kershaw and his daughter, Mr. Dalton, and Lord Chatfield's own brother, Mr. Hargrave.

And yet again, if Mr. Kershaw was correct, and the message had been printed in newspapers and travel guides, anyone could have copied it out and used it.

I tossed and turned, going over the meaning of the mummy, and wondered what the morning would bring.

CHAPTER 17

I awoke the next morning to a magical mist hanging over camp. The mist made its way up from the Nile and through the gateway between the two hills guarding the site. The vaporous tendrils crawled along the sand, clinging to each object, sliding over the tents, and leaving a trail of fine droplets in their wake.

As the sun rose above the hills, its rays hit the mist, and it evaporated in an instant in a puff of smoke, like the trick of a magician.

A silence blanketed the still sleeping camp, and I wondered when the workers would start their daily excavation. Somewhere in the distance, I could hear work resuming at other tombs in the valley, and for a moment I wondered if Mr. Hargrave's laborers had delayed their tasks, and the accompanying clatter and yells, for our benefit.

Then I remembered the mummy. The local men were already anxious about working on the site due to the purported curse. What would they make of the mummy's appearance at the camp in the middle of the night once their brethren had told them about it? Would they refuse to return to their duties on account of it?

As other guests woke up, they seemed reluctant to disturb the peace of the camp. The mood was quite subdued, perhaps troubled by thoughts of the midnight mummy, and Lord Chatfield's death.

Matters were not improved by the arrival of the foreman during breakfast, informing Mr. Hargrave —quite apologetically—that the workers, having learned of the wandering mummy, were asking for higher pay, and were not going to return to work until demands were met.

"That just confirms my opinion," Mrs. Babcock said, sipping her tea. "Indolent and greedy. One wishes one didn't have to rely on the locals for this excavation work."

Mrs. Gladstone nodded in agreement.

"One has to make allowances, Mrs. Babcock," Mr. Hargrave submitted. "It is not the easiest of jobs."

Soon, however, the melancholy of the camp was broken by a tumult of an unexpected kind— braying donkeys and barking dogs. We took to our binoculars to locate the source of the commotion. It was the members of the Royal Society making their way to the dig. The Lords, unfettered by the events of the previous night, had apparently decided to arrive bright and early at the dig.

The procession was a cacophony of Egyptian handlers badgering the emaciated animals carrying the Lords on their backs, accompanied by cries from the Lords themselves, who first spurred the animals on, only to plead for them to slow down when the animals picked up speed. Stray dogs circled the caravan, snapping at the dangling ankles of the Lords. Behind them came the secretaries and valets, carrying excavating apparatus in a dignified manner.

"One presumes that the donkeys would not be so slow to proceed if their path was not impeded by sellers of water, trinkets, and fruits, and by beggars." Mrs. Babcock said. She had joined me to observe the cavalcade.

I studied Mrs. Babcock more closely. Her face was calm and intelligent, but a look of disdain colored her eyes, as though she resented the picture in front of her. I thought back to some of the comments I had heard her make about the dig's workers. For a woman who had spent so much time in Egypt, and was so enamored by ancient Egyptian culture, she struck me as having a very low opinion of the Egyptians themselves. It was as though she felt that it was wrong to have left Egypt to the Egyptians.

As if reading my thoughts, she added. "You know, the Egyptians do not truly care about the ancient Egyptian monuments. To them, these are buildings of heathens. They are only interested in them now because the monuments bring them tourists and money."

I was spared a comment by the arrival of the Royal Society inside the camp. Their appearance lightened the mood and provided some comic relief as we watched valets and donkey owners endeavoring to disentangle Lords and equipment from the animals' backs.

Mr. Hargrave greeted the new arrivals and directed the deposition of their equipment.

I waved to Uncle Albert and joined him.

"A beautiful day for some tomb exploration and beetle gathering," he said by way of greeting.

Mr. Hargrave informed the Lords of the happenings of the previous night, but instead of dampening their enthusiasm, the members of the Royal Society seemed exhilarated by the prospect of some foul play. James gave me a questioning look, and I just shrugged to let him know that all was alright.

And though the absence of workers was perhaps detrimental to Mr. Hargrave's excavation, their truancy allowed us to explore the tomb at leisure.

The time before lunch was taken up by observing the mummy, eliciting cries of delight and disgust, followed by a tour of the part of the tomb that had already been excavated. Exploration was slow going, as all of us had to fit through a rather small hole that functioned as an entrance into the tomb for now, until the whole portal could be excavated.

A long, upwards slanting corridor, painted with scarabs, much to the delight of the Lords, led to a wooden door. Behind the door was the antechamber. It was surprisingly sparse.

"We are now inside those rocky cliffs you saw bordering the camp," Mr. Hargrave said.

Another hole had been made into the thick stone wall on the right.

"That's the burial chamber," he continued, squeezing through the hole. We followed him into a small chamber, illuminated only by the lamp in Mr. Hargrave's hand, containing a stone sarcophagus. "This is where we found the mummy." His voice echoed around the empty room.

Located so deep inside the rocky outcrops, the chamber was cool. But with all the living bodies now gathered in it, it began to feel stuffy. Some of the Lords moved back out into the antechamber, where Mrs. Gladstone, unable to make it through the hole, had remained with her companion.

"Does this tomb contain a treasury?" Mr. Kershaw asked, looking around.

"You mean like the one in Tutankhamen's tomb? No, not that we've been able to find," Mr. Hargrave said and shook his head. "Our man, Ahmose, was not a pharaoh, after all. But these writings here,"—he illuminated some of the hieroglyphs on the wall—"refer to the temple of Khepri I was telling you about. And its riches."

The archeologists gathered around Mr. Hargrave's lamp, Miss Kershaw quite close by his side, and studied the drawings and carvings on the wall. These were exceptionally well preserved —bright, colorful, and crisp. My heart beat faster, just thinking of the joy and elation one must feel upon first discovering such a place.

"Could the temple be in another chamber from here?" Mr. Kershaw asked, tapping the walls of the chamber optimistically.

"We've probed the walls, but all beyond this chamber sounds solid. Plus, there are no cuts in the rock that would indicate there was anything other than just solid rock behind it." We gazed at the smooth walls of the chamber with some disappointment. "And one can't ask the workers to dig tunnels into solid rock indefinitely if one has no indication of where the secret temple might be."

"But wouldn't there be some sort of above-ground structure, some remnant that would show where a temple might have been?" Miss Kershaw asked.

"We have exhausted this avenue of investigation," Mr. Hargrave said. "The ancient Egyptians had a tendency to build over the temples of previous generations, as beliefs shifted and different deities gained importance. To that end, we have examined the foundations of many of the temples in this valley, but to no avail."

"But you have to remember, Mr. Hargrave," Mr. Kershaw broke in, "that a temple devoted to Khepri would have been a clandestine operation, at best. The cult of Khepri was not an officially sanctioned cult by the Pharaoh. And even though this high priest, Ahmose, was the Pharaoh's brother, he still would have feared the Pharaoh's wrath, death even. Any of his fellow priests would have gladly given him away if they'd learned of his cult. So, most likely, the temple would be found underground or carved into the rocks."

Mr. Hargrave nodded as though he had not considered this possibility, and Mr. Dalton looked disappointed. His talk on the boat had left me with the impression that he was here to buy whatever was dug up from this temple of Khepri. With no temple located, he would have a long time to wait.

"Why would Ahmose start a new cult, if it was so dangerous?" I asked.

"History tells us that new cults arise as a way to usurp some of the power and influence of the established religion. Perhaps even for financial gain, through the offerings made to the new temple," Mr. Hargrave said. "However, Ahmose seems to have truly had visions of Khepri, as this series of hieroglyphs attests." He moved his lantern over another section of the wall, dominated by a man with a beetle head. "The message of Khepri is one of rebirth and eternal life."

"*Lapis philosophorum*. The philosopher's stone," Mr. Dalton said, his eyes dancing over the paintings on the wall. "The elixir of life. Stone of immortality."

"Not alchemy again, Mr. Dalton," Mr. Kershaw said with a groan.

"That is a very limited view to take," Mr. Dalton countered. "The ancient Egyptians had plenty of gold. But everlasting life had eluded them. Everything in the ancient Egyptian religion was about rebirth and continuing to live in the next life—the mummies, the careful preservation of organs in canopic jars, the Book of the Dead that gave instructions on what to expect after death and supplied spells to use in the underworld on the way to paradise. Overcoming death and attaining immortality in the next life, was what the ancient Egyptians were after."

I watched Mr. Dalton with interest. He was quite knowledgeable for a man who was not a trained archeologist. But perhaps a successful antiques dealer had to be.

"The element of greed attached to the philosopher's stone," Mr. Dalton continued, "the notion of a stone that turns base metals into gold, was a Renaissance conceit."

The conversation flowed naturally from the question of everlasting life to lunch, and we resurfaced from the tomb—much like a beetle crawling out of its burrow—into the bright sunshine, to find lunch waiting for us. We took our seats in safari chairs, under a broad tent canopy, to a feast catered by the Swiss chef at The Winter Palace Hotel.

Though the following day was to be devoted entirely to beetle hunting with an excursion to the desert beyond Luxor, it appeared that Lord Mantelbury could not resist following a beetle that caught his attention around the tent. Soon, all the Lords of the Royal Society were bumbling about, eyes glued to the ground, bumping into tables and chairs, looking under people's feet, searching for beetles.

The hunt soon extended over the entire camp.

"What is that pile over there?" Uncle Albert asked Mr. Hargrave excitedly, pointing to a pile of what looked like stone and whatnot to one side of the tomb. "Is it rubbish? Beetles love rubbish."

"Yes, it's where the workers bury refuse. Though it still tends to attract wild animals."

Uncle Albert perked up. "Really? Why, that's a perfect place for beetles! They love any place with decaying matter." He nodded appreciatively in the direction of the mound. "Cover me, Caroline," he whispered to me. "I'm going to explore. But don't let the other ruffians see what I'm doing."

Uncle Albert set off on his mission. But his attempt at a clandestine operation was met with some resistance by the gods. He kept tripping and bumping into things, so that by the time he reached the dump, most of the members of the Royal Society had joined him.

In an attempt to distance himself from them, Uncle Albert moved further away, towards some high rocks on the outskirts of the site. He was following a beetle most doggedly, though I was paying little attention to him, thinking of my own matters, and James.

"I say!" my uncle exclaimed from the other end of the camp. "What rotten luck! I rather fancied that one."

I smiled at my uncle's childish frustration.

"There goes another one!" my uncle declared again.

I moved in my uncle's direction to see what the shouting was about. His cries had attracted the attention of the other people in the camp.

"What is it?" I said.

"Beetles are disappearing into this hole," he said, pointing crossly at a small opening in the ground. Without waiting for my reply, he started digging with an energy that seemed to be fueled by the frustration of being deprived of a particularly fine beetle specimen.

The hole was growing bigger by the minute. I looked at Mr. Hargrave, who was watching the proceedings with interest. His face had assumed a curious look, and then comprehension spread across it.

"Lord Tatham," he addressed my uncle. "I say! I

think it might be better if I took over."

But just as he was saying that, the sand under my uncle gave way and he tumbled down into the abyss.

CHAPTER 18

"Uncle!" I cried, kneeling and thrusting my head into the uncle-sized hole in the ground. "Are you alright?"

"I'm quite alright, my child," floated my uncle's feeble voice. "Knocked the wind out of me a bit, but I seemed to be unharmed. I chanced a rather soft landing," he added.

Wilford, who had raced over upon Uncle's cry, replaced me at the hole. "Shall I come down to fetch you, My Lord?"

"No need, Wilford. I'm perfectly fine down here."

"Fetch a ladder," Mr. Hargrave instructed the private secretaries.

"I don't need a ladder," Uncle Albert's defiant voice floated up through the hole. I wondered if he'd found some nice beetles he was trying to hide from the rest of the Royal Society. And yet, it sounded as though there was an echo in the hole. "Perhaps a lamp would not go amiss," my uncle added. "I have a feeling this shaft is quite big."

By now, the ladder had arrived and was lowered

into the hole, conveying Mr. Hargrave with a lamp.

"I say!" Mr. Hargrave's voice erupted from the opening.

"Is everything alright?" I asked, concerned for Uncle Albert. "Is my uncle unharmed?"

"Oh, Lord Tatham is quite alright! He seems to have landed on a cushion of sand. Sand that must have seeped over millennia through that crevice he found. It's rather like a slide. I daresay there are stairs buried under the sand, leading down from the hole."

"Yes, it was tremendous fun," Uncle Albert called. "For a moment, I felt like a young boy again."

"Mr. Hargrave," Mrs. Babcock leaned in. "Is there anything I could do to help? Shall I dispatch one of the men to fetch some help from the hotel?"

"No, no need Mrs. Babcock," said Mr. Hargrave. "But perhaps you could lower down my kit of tools. There seems to be a door here."

"A door!" Mrs. Babcock exclaimed and quickly looked around for someone to delegate the job to. With all the workers gone, she communicated with some of the donkey owners who were still around, and instructed them where to find Mr. Hargrave's tools.

"I'll go," Mr. Kershaw said, taking charge of the donkey owners.

"May I come down, Mr. Hargrave?" Mrs. Babcock asked.

"No. You'd better stay up there. There isn't much room," he replied to her visible annoyance. She turned red, and touched the tendrils of her hair nervously.

"I say, Caroline. Can you hear me?" Uncle Albert called up, part of his face visible through the hole as he peered up into the light. "It's rather chilly down here. And there is a big seal on the door with a beetle engraved on it."

"Is there a cartouche sealing the door?" Mrs. Babcock asked, her voice betraying her excitement.

"Yes, Mrs. Babcock," answered Mr. Hargrave.

"Is it unbroken?" Miss Kershaw asked. While always cool and detached, even she was circling the opening with nervous energy.

"Yes, Miss Kershaw!" the rejoicing voice of Mr. Hargrave floated up through the hole. "I daresay you would know what that means!"

"The tools," Mr. Kershaw yelled and lowered the basket of hammers and chisels he had brought through the opening.

"Don't you think we should wait? Call some government administrator, or something?" asked Lord Mantelbury, though he delivered the question rather feebly, as though he felt someone should say something official, but didn't enjoy it being him.

"Oh, don't be such a stick in the mud," said Miss Kershaw irreverently, and Lord Mantelbury shrank back.

"Someone go get the foreman! He's gone home for lunch," Mr. Hargrave instructed.

In no time locals and even hotel guests—who had heard the news from a porter, who had heard it from a man working in the kitchens, whose cousin was one of the donkey owners—had gathered around the hole.

A crowd had now collected, and some of the more intrepid onlookers began helping haul sand out of the hole. The top of the opening expanded as we looked on. The foreman tried to keep some semblance of order, but the curiosity of the ever-increasing crowd was difficult to contain. Some of the water and fruit sellers had set up shop along the boundaries of the camp.

Arguing that I had to stay close to the excavation, since Uncle Albert was still underground and refused to leave—who could blame him—I had a front-row seat to the action. For a long while, all there was were bucketfuls of sand. It was rather extraordinary how much sand there was everywhere and how even a small crevice, like the one my uncle had spied, could allow for so much sand to accumulate over the ages.

Afternoon tea was forgotten by all except the cynical Lords, who proceeded back to the hotel, much to the renewed regret of their secretaries and the owners of their appointed donkeys.

Unfortunately for James, Lord Packenham was one of the unbelievers.

As the stairway was cleared, a camera was lowered for Mr. Hargrave to take a photograph of the door and the seal, before he opened it.

The sun was moving lower still in the sky and the shadows aboveground were getting longer. Soon it would dip behind the hills. A sense of anticipation permeated the gathered crowd. We were all captivated by the sound of Mr. Hargrave's chisel striking against stone, and peered down, as far as light would permit, towards the door.

I took the opportunity of a momentary lapse in the foreman's attention to glide down the stairs to my uncle's side. Mr. Kershaw and his daughter, followed by Mr. Dalton, Mrs. Gladstone, and Miss Parker, slipped down the stairs after me. Even Mrs. Babcock, after many insincere objections, disregarded the foreman's pleas and joined us.

Only Wilford, the remaining donkey owners, and the hotel visitors displayed some sense of decorum by remaining on the surface. They peered into the opening with their heads silhouetted against the sky.

I mused that the purported curse and dire warnings seemed to have been forgotten by all from our boat party.

As the door was taken off its hinges—"To preserve the seal," Mr. Hargrave had said—a cold blast met us. A collective shiver traveled through the group, as though we were at Mrs. Gladstone's seance once again. I wondered if it was the cold, or some primal fear which shook us. Mrs. Gladstone, for all her spiritual posturing, crossed herself.

A dark hole gaped beyond the door.

"More light," Mr. Hargrave called and lanterns were handed down.

Mr. Hargrave stepped boldly into the darkness. And as each of us got a hold of a lantern, each of us ventured, unbidden, down the corridor that had opened up behind the door.

An overwhelming sense of awe overtook me. We were the first people to set foot here in thousands of years. I held on to Uncle Albert and he leaned into me. His face was a reflection of my own wonderment.

The air was stale, but that did not detract from the magnificent paintings on the wall—as bright and fresh as though they were painted not long ago. Fresher than the frescoes at the Vatican. The length of the corridor was lined with row upon row of hieroglyphs. Some of the archeologists lingered to make sense of them.

"This looks like it's freshly painted!" Miss Parker, whose voice we rarely heard, objected with disbelief.

"I assure you, miss," said Mr. Hargrave with some pride in his voice, "this is thousands of years old."

And yet, at first glance, I could understand Miss

Parker's disbelief.

We came to a split in the corridor, and then another, and soon it seemed as though each of us was walking down a different passageway.

"It's like a labyrinth!" I heard Miss Kershaw exclaim from somewhere down and to the left of us.

I walked beside Uncle Albert, holding out our lantern in front of us.

"Did you notice the scarab on the seal?" Uncle Albert asked in a hushed tone, though we were quite alone.

I nodded. I'd had the same thought. I'd also begun to wonder if perhaps this was the Temple of Khepri, the beetle-headed incarnation of the god Ra that Mr. Hargrave had been looking for.

But the wall paintings around us were much like what we had seen in other tombs and temples in Egypt, only with the occasional extra scarab thrown in.

We entered another arm of the maze, and soon ended in what seemed like a circular space. It was too small to be a room and seemed more like an antechamber.

I heard Uncle Albert squeal softly, but whether with delight or fear, I could not tell.

"Raise the light," he urged. "Something interesting is on the walls."

I had seen Uncle Albert this excited only once

on the trip, and it wasn't over Egyptian art. It was when he'd caught sight of, and subsequently lost, an uncommonly shiny beetle.

But as I raised the lantern, I didn't have to wonder long about the reason behind my aged relation's excitement. The walls of this antechamber were covered in depictions of golden scarabs in the most singular fashion.

Uncle Albert and I stood there gazing at the paintings, and I wondered if he realized what we were seeing.

I glanced quickly at his head. "Are you wearing the new fez you acquired in Cairo?"

"Yes, why?"

"Do you remember the lining?" I asked, somewhat exasperated.

"Yes, it was rather a nice touch, that," he said and slipped the fez off.

I took it from his hands. "Where is the lining, Uncle Albert?!" I exclaimed. The fez was naked on the inside.

"Oh, that," he said, unperturbed. "I had to cut that away. The silk made the fez quite slippery, and it threatened to fall off my head more than once. Wilford suggested removing it, most helpfully."

"Yes, but don't you see? The lining matched the pattern of this room!" I exclaimed. I then looked around sheepishly, wondering if anyone had heard us. "Where is the lining now?" I asked, my voice quivering with dread.

"Now what did I do with it?" Uncle Albert said, patting his hands up and down his suit. "Now, I wonder if that was what the rascals were after?"

"What rascals?" I said, my dread turning to concern.

"My cabin on the boat had been rifled through one day," he said, in a matter-of-fact tone. "Or perhaps it was during the night..."

"When? Why didn't you tell me?" I protested.

"I didn't want to worry you. And since nothing seemed to have been taken, I didn't say anything."

What was the meaning of all this? Who had gone through my uncle's things, and was it the fez's lining that they had been looking for? Is this why the man with the scar had followed us to the boat? And who on the boat was working with him?

Instinctively I looked back, to see if anyone had overheard us. Had that person followed us in here? But I only saw darkness.

"Now, where did Wilford put it?" Uncle Albert was checking each of his pockets. "Or perhaps it's in my other suit..."

Even without the lining on hand, however, it was clear that the designs embroidered on it looked very much like the surrounding walls—dark blue with golden scarabs.

"Now, how did the old fez-maker come to see this room?" Uncle Albert wondered aloud.

How, indeed?

But before we could contemplate the mystery of Uncle Albert's fez, a blood-curdling scream reverberated through the underground tunnels.

CHAPTER 19

The cry sent a shiver down my spine, and suddenly I felt quite cold.

"A ghost?" Uncle Albert wondered.

I grabbed him by the elbow without answering. Fear and curiosity, and the need to be with other living souls, propelled my feet towards the scream. Though I could not be certain where it had come from, I could hear people running down the arms of the labyrinth. And when we got to the central corridor, I could see that they were all moving in the same direction.

But Uncle Albert was not an athlete, and we were the last people to arrive at the place where everyone had gathered.

The lanterns in people's hands illuminated a body lying on the ground. It was Mr. Hargrave.

A large rock lay beside him. I peered closer. A dark stain in the sand told me that his head was bleeding. Miss Kershaw, her lamp discarded to the side, was standing over him, sobbing uncontrollably.

"Oh, dear child," Mr. Kershaw hurried by his

daughter's side and hugged her. Her sobs shook her body as she turned to weep into his chest.

We all stared, immobilized by surprise and shock, at Miss Kershaw and Mr. Hargrave for a few moments.

Unbidden, my mind reflected on how one never really knew people, especially not after spending a short time with them on a boat. I would have not expected Miss Kershaw to react so forcefully to Mr. Hargrave's death. She hadn't behaved like this upon Lord Chatfield's death. But perhaps the events of the last few days—the seance, the mummy, the unexpected discovery of these underground chambers, and now Mr. Hargrave's accident—were too much for her to handle.

"Is he dead?" Mr. Dalton asked and kneeled beside Mr. Hargrave, checking for a pulse. He shook his head as he looked up at us. "That rock must have fallen from there and hit him on the head." Mr. Dalton pointed to a crumbling column near Mr. Hargrave's body.

It was then that I first noticed the chamber we were standing in. Though our lanterns cast their light only on part of the space, it was clear that the chamber resembled a large hall, with columns running throughout, not unlike a cathedral. Our small group spread out for a moment, examining the pillars. Many of the columns were crumbling, just like the one Mr. Dalton had pointed to. Large chunks of stone lay at the base of a number of them.

As we moved our lamps about, golden scarabs glinted from the walls. And now a statue in the center of the hall became visible. It was the beetle god Khepri. This looked to be the central chamber of this underground structure.

"What a tragic accident," Mrs. Babcock said.

"It's the curse!" Mrs. Gladstone shrieked, making us all jump. "Take me up, Daisy," she said to Miss Parker and leaned heavily on her arm. "I feel faint. I need fresh air. Even though there is no fresh air in all of Egypt," she lamented and lumbered away with Miss Parker's support.

I wondered if Mrs. Gladstone should not stay. After all, this was a death, and we needed to establish the details of how Mr. Hargrave met his end before we all scattered.

A male voice in the central corridor, however, stopped me from calling Mrs. Gladstone back. She re-entered our chamber, followed by Mr. Lowell, the British official.

I wondered where he had come from.

"What is going on here?!" Mr. Lowell shouted. "Who has given you authorization to come down here? You have broken a number of local laws!"

He stared around at our blank faces.

"What are you doing here, Mr. Lowell?" I asked. I wondered what had brought him down to us. Had the people above heard Miss Kershaw's cry?

"News of the discovery reached me, as these things do in Egypt, and I came to close the site off until the Egyptian officials from the Department of Antiquities can get here...Why are you all looking at me that way? Where is Mr. Hargrave? I need to speak to him about this irregularity—"

We had moved out of the way, and Mr. Lowell saw Mr. Hargrave's body on the ground.

"What's happened?!" Mr. Lowell cried. "Why did no one tell me?!" He bounded to the body and leaned down to examine him. "What happened?" he asked again, looking at each of us in turn.

We looked at each other, as though no one knew what exactly had happened.

"One of us should go get help," Mr. Dalton said and made to leave.

Mr. Lowell blocked his progress with a bound. "No one is leaving here before I understand what has happened," he said with a menacing note in his voice. "There is not much anyone can do to help Mr. Hargrave now," he added more kindly.

"What are your credentials?" asked Mr. Dalton in a correspondingly threatening tone. "I am an American citizen. You have no right to detain me."

"I think you will find me rather easier to deal with than the Egyptian police, Mr. Dalton." Mr. Lowell glared at the American. "Especially with your background," he added with a meaningful look. "The Department of Antiquities will not look kindly on your trespass here." He then turned to the rest of us. "All of you. The Egyptians will not be happy."

He spoke with such authority that none other dared object, and yet I noticed that he had not answered Mr. Dalton's question about his exact official role in Egypt.

"We entered here under the guidance and authority of Mr. Hargrave," said Mrs. Gladstone, defiantly.

I thought that was rather stretching the truth. Mr. Hargrave had not given us express permission to enter. But he had not stopped us either.

"Mr. Hargrave is now, sadly, dead," countered Mr. Lowell. "As a representative of the British government, I have some sway with officials here. Let us go over what happened. That way, you can be prepared for when the police question you."

"If I may be of some assistance," Mrs. Babcock spoke up with a self-control that was admirable under the circumstances.

"Yes?" Mr. Lowell looked at her questioningly. "In what way could you assist?"

"As you know, I am, was, Mr. Hargrave's secretary. If you have any questions about the operation here, you can direct them to me. I have been thoroughly involved in the decisions made at the dig."

"Are you saying that you take responsibility for this tomb raid?" Mr. Lowell challenged her.

Mrs. Babcock did not falter under his stern look.

I speculated that she was used to standing her ground with men.

"I make no such claims, as you well know," Mrs. Babcock said. "All I am saying is that following the death of Lord Chatfield, and now his brother's, I am the one who is most familiar with their affairs. I see myself as the one in charge of the site at the moment. I was...I was quite close to them."

"My condolences," Mr. Lowell said. Mrs. Babcock received them with a nod. "But I am sure, madam, that you understand that the dig site, following the concession holder's death, will be taken over by the authorities, and the concession will be allotted to another archaeological team."

"Yes, I am well aware that I am out of a job now that both brothers are dead," she said with an injured tone but head held high. "I was merely being civil and offering my help." She looked away.

The British official's expression softened. "I am certain your expertise will be highly sought after, especially by the next holder of the concession. And you will be the first person I turn to if any questions regarding Mr. Hargrave's business affairs arise in the course of our investigation. Now," he turned to the rest of us. "Did anyone see what happened?" All pleasantness was gone from his face, replaced by a mask of British civil servant efficiency.

No one replied.

"Who discovered Mr. Hargrave?" Mr. Lowell

tried again.

"Miss Kershaw, I think," came Miss Parker's uncertain voice.

"Did you see anything, Miss Kershaw?" he turned to her.

She shook her head, still buried in her father's shirt, and sobbed.

"Did anyone hear anything?" Mr. Lowell asked.

"Well, there was Miss Kershaw's scream," Mrs. Babcock said. "It brought us all here."

"I heard a heavy thud," Mrs. Gladstone interjected. "It must have been the falling rock. It was at least a few minutes before the scream."

Mr. Lowell nodded. "So then Miss Kershaw screamed when she found the body? Is that correct, Miss Kershaw?"

"Leave her alone," Mr. Kershaw roared. But his daughter lifted her head and nodded. Her eyes were swollen and red.

Mr. Lowell noted something down in a notebook he'd pulled out of his coat. "Looking at the state of the columns in this room, I believe we can conclude this was an accident. But just to be sure of no foul play, we need to establish where everyone was when they heard the scream?"

"It's hard to tell, in a corridor somewhere," Mr. Dalton said.

The rest assented.

"There are so many of them here," Mrs. Babcock

added.

I took the opportunity to frown meaningfully at my uncle, to warn him not to reveal our exact location. But he just smiled at me beatifically, which did not reassure me in the least.

"Right," Mr. Lowell continued. "Can anyone confirm where you were prior to the scream? Were some of you perhaps in the company of others?"

"What are you insinuating, Mr. Lowell?!" Mrs. Babcock asked, outraged. "Are you asking us for an alibi?"

"I am simply trying to establish how Mr. Hargrave's death came about. It could have been an accident, or it could have been brought on by someone."

"It's just as you predicted, Mrs. Gladstone," Mr. Dalton said with some malice in his voice.

The woman sent him a deadly glare.

"What is this?" Mr. Lowell asked.

"We had a seance on the boat," Mr. Dalton said. "Mrs. Gladstone predicted more deaths to come!" The antiques dealer glared at Mrs. Gladstone in return, as though challenging her to contradict him.

"That's not what I meant. I was—" Mrs. Gladstone stopped abruptly as though she did not want to say what she had meant by her prediction.

"Where were you, Mrs. Gladstone, when you heard the scream?"

"I was with my companion, Miss Parker."

"Actually, I saw you walking in this general direction by yourself, just prior to the scream," interrupted Mr. Dalton.

"How could you be sure it was me in the darkness of this place?" Mrs. Gladstone shot back.

Mr. Dalton simply cast a quick glance at Mrs. Gladstone's hat, but did not verbalize his apparent thought—no one else here wore quite such an ostentatious hat. It would be difficult to mistake, even in the gloom of the underground corridors.

"Miss," Mr. Lowell turned to Miss Parker. "Can you confirm Mrs. Gladstone's whereabouts at the time of the accident?"

"Hey, why aren't you asking anyone else about their alibi?" protested Mrs. Gladstone, quite unladylike. "Why are you picking on me?"

"All in good time, Mrs. Gladstone. I will get to all the gathered here. Now Miss Parker, was Mrs. Gladstone with you the whole time, as she claims?"

"Yes. But she left me for a few moments," Miss Parker said in a timid voice and glanced anxiously at her employer. "She went down a corridor...I didn't see her again until we met here."

Mrs. Gladstone scowled at her companion, but as the realization that she was caught out in a lie dawned on her, she looked around in desperation.

"But before reaching this place, she ran into me," said Mrs. Babcock. "Isn't that right, Mrs.

Gladstone?"

I thought Mrs. Gladstone hesitated for a moment. "Yes, that's right. Mrs. Babcock and I entered here together."

Uncle Albert stepped forward. "I was with my niece, Caroline, in the—" he halted abruptly. I had pinched him hard in order to make him keep quiet, or at least to lose his train of thought. It worked.

"I have no one to vouch for my whereabouts," Mr. Dalton volunteered boldly. "And I don't need to. But anyhow, I arrived after the women."

"My daughter and I were together...but then we also got separated," said Mr. Kershaw. He faltered and his brow furrowed, as though he was going over something in his head.

Mr. Lowell nodded. "So, except for Lady Caroline and her uncle, and Mrs. Babcock and Mrs. Gladstone, no one else has anyone to vouch for their whereabouts when Mr. Hargrave met his death."

A murmur of dissent passed through the crowd, but no one contradicted his statement.

After a few more questions, Mr. Lowell escorted us to the exit of the tomb.

Uncle Albert, having stood on his feet for so long, had some trouble getting going, so we were quite behind everyone else as we made our way out.

Then, Mrs. Gladstone's voice came from quite near us. Perhaps Mrs. Gladstone, who was quite slow herself, had not realized that Uncle Albert and I were behind the corner from her. Whatever the reason, I clearly heard her hissing at her companion: "What is going on here, Daisy? That's not the right death."

CHAPTER 20

Twilight had enveloped the dig site as we made our way out. Men with donkeys were waiting for us, each carrying a lantern.

As I rode back to the hotel by my uncle's side, I had plenty of time to go over what had happened underground. Uncle Albert, proclaiming that the most interesting insects were to be found at dusk, stopped off every few paces to examine some winged or crawling beast.

While I was certain we had inadvertently discovered the long-forgotten Temple of Ahmose that Mr. Hargrave had been looking for, it was Mr. Hargrave's death that occupied my mind.

Was it not strange that Mrs. Gladstone had predicted another death, and that only a few days later, someone who had attended her seance was dead?

How could the woman have foretold such a thing? Could Mr. Hargrave's death really be an accident? And who had tampered with the mummy the previous night?

I let the donkey carry me towards the hotel

and cast my mind back over all that had occurred during our boat ride up the Nile.

First, there had been the story of the curse and treasure. Soon after, Lord Chatfield had died. Had the story of the curse given someone the idea of a clever way to eliminate Lord Chatfield? *But no, that could not be right!* I chastised myself. *Lord Chatfield's death was an accident!*

Or was it? My mind jumped back to another drowning death I had witnessed not long ago. I shook the pesky thought away. *No!* We had all seen Lord Chatfield get pulled under the water by a crocodile. He was unlikely to have survived. And yet, his body had not been found. I pushed that thought aside for the moment.

Had someone skillfully manipulated Lord Chatfield into exploring the river bank at dusk, knowing full well the dangers? Was there someone among our boat party who had been well-aware of Lord Chatfield's deficits of character? Had someone exploited his tendency to be prideful and rash?

But surely, hoping Lord Chatfield would get attacked by a crocodile at dusk was an inefficient way to get rid of him, fraught with uncertainty and ripe for failure?

I tried to recall how Lord Chatfield's fatal excursion had come to pass. But all I could remember was that he got into some sort of argument with his brother and then went ashore. I was quite certain he had not been manipulated by anyone into doing such a foolish thing.

So then, was Mr. Hargrave to blame for his brother's death? He'd had a lot to gain by it—a title and control over the dig concession. He had been the better archeologist, but had lived in his brother's shadow. He'd let his brother take all the glory, simply because his brother had the money.

Plus, Lord Chatfield had been ghastly to Mr. Hargrave. He'd threatened cutting off funding for the dig at every opportunity. Lord Chatfield hadn't seemed to care all that much about Egyptology. Perhaps he really was going to suspend funding for the dig, and Mr. Hargrave had found a way to stop him. I made a mental note to ask Mrs. Babcock if there was any veracity to Lord Chatfield's threats, or whether they had been deployed to irritate his younger brother most effectively.

But now that Mr. Hargrave himself was dead, his motives, and any hand he might have had in his brother's death, were surely futile points to investigate.

I corralled my thoughts back to the events on the boat. After Lord Chatfield's death, there had been the seance and the first time the advent of another death was mentioned. Mrs. Gladstone cried "curse!" every chance she got, but she had mentioned the death only once.

Then there had been the mummy at the camp, with another warning about the curse and of a death to come. But I could not be entirely certain that it had been Mrs. Gladstone's doing. For one thing, was Mrs. Gladstone strong enough to carry a mummy? How heavy was a mummy, anyway? Here was another thing I needed to look into.

Lastly, there had been Mr. Hargrave's death in the temple. It was the culmination of all the talk about curses and death.

And while Mrs. Gladstone's ability to predict death was quite astounding, it was her reaction to Mr. Hargrave's death that I found most intriguing. Why did she tell her companion that the wrong person had died? Was this not a remark only a killer would make? Was she admitting that she had killed Mr. Hargrave by mistake?

The darkness in the tomb had been impenetrable, unless one carried a lantern. And though she eventually met with Mrs. Babcock, Mr. Dalton had seen Mrs. Gladstone wandering towards where Mr. Hargrave was found. Mrs. Gladstone could have had plenty of time to hit him on the head with one of the fallen rocks and then to backtrack to another corridor.

But if she had killed Mr. Hargrave by mistake, then who was the intended victim? And were more deaths to come?

And if she were the killer, why had she made such an elaborate announcement about the intended death? Why had she drawn so much attention to herself? Would it not have been more cunning to kill without all these theatrics?

I stopped myself. Why was I assuming that Mr. Hargrave was killed? Had not Mr. Lowell, and everyone else, concluded that his death was an accident?

Was the unnatural prediction of death making me think that there was foul play here?

What possible motive could Mrs. Gladstone—who, according to her, had never left New York—have for killing Mr. Hargrave? By all indications, they had never met? Or, if his death had been a mistake, who was she really after? Was she after someone she had met in New York? Mr. Dalton was an American. And Miss Kershaw had studied in New York. Perhaps Mr. Kershaw had gone to New York as well to visit his daughter and had run into Mrs. Gladstone while there. But none of these passengers had shown any sign of recognition of Mrs. Gladstone.

Whatever her motivations might have been, it seemed to me, however, that Mrs. Gladstone did not have an alibi for the time of Mr. Hargrave's death.

Why had Mrs. Babcock been so eager to provide her with one? Was it perhaps because Mrs. Babcock herself did not have an alibi? And yet, what would Mrs. Babcock's motive be for killing Mr. Hargrave? With both brothers dead, she was out of a job. And there was no guarantee that she would be employed by the next concession holder. Was Mrs.

Babcock perhaps hoping to get the concession herself? But surely that was unlikely. From the little I had seen of Egypt and the way it operated, the Department of Antiquities was unlikely to offer the concession to a woman.

So Mrs. Gladstone and Mrs. Babcock did not have an alibi for the time of Mr. Hargrave's death, I concluded. But neither did any of the other members of the group. Mr. Dalton had seen Mrs. Gladstone walking in the direction of where Mr. Hargrave had been found. But if he had seen her, that meant that he was in the right area at the right time as well. And Mr. Kershaw and his daughter didn't have alibis either.

I could just make out Miss Kershaw, at the head of our donkey caravan. She was working her donkey the hardest, willing it to go faster. Why was she in such a hurry to get back to the hotel?

I heard again Miss Kershaw's scream in my mind. Why had she reacted so forcefully to Mr. Hargrave's death? Had she seen who had killed him? But she had denied any such knowledge. Was she protecting her father, perhaps?

So, at the time of Mr. Hargrave's death, each of these people was wandering the labyrinth-like corridors of the temple without a witness. And each had just as much of a motive for killing Mr. Hargrave as Mrs. Gladstone. Mr. Kershaw could hope to get his hands on the concession now that Mr. Hargrave was out of the way. Mr. Dalton, now that the temple was discovered, could hope to get at the purported treasure...

"Of course!" I cried out and made my donkey handler jump. *Why had I not seen it before?*

Surely the discovery of the temple of the beetle-headed deity was the reason behind Mr. Hargrave's death! The dig concession now was much more valuable than it had been this morning. It not only contained the tomb of the high priest but also the secret temple he had built.

And the value of the dig was nothing to the treasure the temple contained, if the legend was true! Who would not commit a murder for a chance to attain immeasurable wealth and the secret to eternal life?

Treasure, curses, death. Where did the truth lie?

I let my mind wander over the possibilities of what was hidden inside the temple. Was it indeed possible that Uncle Albert's fez was connected to these mysteries somehow? Did someone really go through Uncle Albert's things on the boat? Were they looking for his fez? Was a hidden message contained in the lining?

I shook my head. Perhaps the decorations on the temple's walls, like the tomb curses, were ones that had been used in many places before. Perhaps golden scarabs against a blue background were just a folk decorative element used since the ancient Egyptians.

What would happen now that the secret temple had been discovered? If someone had murdered Mr. Hargrave for access to the temple, was Uncle, or at least his fez, in danger? Would I see the man with the scar again? And would we ever get another chance to explore the temple and its mysteries?

Surrounded by the manifestations of the ancient Egyptians—the magnificent pharaoh tombs buried deep in the eternal sands behind me, and the grand temples of Luxor just visible in the purple twilight ahead of me—it seemed quite possible that such things as curses, treasures, and secret ciphers that unlocked the mysteries of eternal life, were indeed real.

But if the ancient Egyptians had discovered the secret to eternal life, one had to concede that it had not done them much good. I cast a glance at the opened tombs gaping from the cliffs.

I rode on, making an effort to keep my feet up off the ground and prevent my shoes from dragging in the sand. Truthfully, one was much better off walking, but providing donkey transport seemed to be one of the few ways to make a living in Egypt, and I was not about to deny a job to any man. I ruffled the donkey's rough mane running down its back. Poor beasts.

Our hotel was visible in the distance, glowing from within against the darkening sky. It looked like a magnificent mirage of lights and lush palms in the desolate sands.

Upon crossing the Nile, I noticed that Poppy's sailboat had finally arrived, and was moored not far from the hotel. I planned to send a note to her upon reaching the hotel.

But as we entered the hotel, much later than anyone else, as Uncle Albert had stopped to look at some infernal moth attacking an exotic blossom in the hotel's garden, I could see that something important had transpired.

Men in crumpled linen suits and dusty hats, which unmistakably singled them out as journalists, were gathered in the lobby. But so was everyone from the temple.

There, on a sofa in the lobby, lay Mrs. Gladstone. Miss Parker was sitting by her side, attempting to revive her. My first thought was that Mrs. Gladstone herself had been attacked. But then I noticed the hovering hotel attendants, offering glasses of water and fans in turn.

"What has happened?" I asked no one in particular.

"The dame fainted. She just received a telegram from New York that her husband has kicked the bucket," one of the journalists put it most eloquently.

CHAPTER 21

By the next morning, the hotel had become insufferable.

Following Lord Chatfield's accident, the world press had begun circling the hotel, awaiting the arrival of our boat, as the concierge had informed me. Now, the journalists had gathered in throngs in the lobby, outdoing each other filing reports on the Curse of the Scarab, as they had christened the events. They could not get enough of the deaths that had occurred in such a quick succession—Lord Chatfield's uncle, Lord Chatfield, Mr. Hargrave, and now, Mr. Gladstone in New York —and were merrily predicting who might be next.

Mrs. Gladstone and her companion had left this morning to make their way to Alexandria and from there on the next cross-Atlantic boat to New York. Miss Parker had taken great pains to shield her employer from the intrusive journalists and photographers, though Mrs. Gladstone's enormous hat had done an excellent job of protecting her grief-stricken face.

The Curse of the Scarab overshadowed even news coming out of the Tutankhamen tomb, which Mr. Carter religiously continued pinning daily to the hotel's bulletin board.

Bolstered by the stream of ominous news coming out of Egypt, punters in Britain were purportedly placing bets on who would die next, and Uncle Albert sent a quick telegram to his Ascot bookmaker, to place a few bets on the other members of the Royal Society. I wanted to point out to him that they were unlikely to be the curse's next victims, as they had not been at the opening of the temple, but I didn't want to spoil his fun.

"Appraising these events in a scientific manner," Lord Packenham pronounced pompously at breakfast, "the most likely succeeding casualty should be Bertie." He cast a gleeful look at Uncle Albert. "He was the one to discover this temple, regardless of how inadvertently." He smirked again in my uncle's direction. And since it appeared that the thought had just occurred to him, he dispatched James to send a telegram to his London bookmaker.

But all these deaths were detracting from the real purpose of the Royal Society's stay in Egypt. The dung beetle competition could not be postponed even for the death of Mr. Hargrave, and the planned excursion to the desert proceeded without interruption.

"Do you think he'll make it?" Poppy asked. She was sitting next to me on a lounger under a canvas marquee, employed to keep us out of the midday sun.

The question was spoken as she looked on to where her husband, Leopold, was blundering about in the sand alongside the members of the Royal Society. Leopold, as a way of testing his abilities and initiating him into the Society's ways, had been assigned to assist Uncle Albert, thus freeing me to sit in the shade. James, poor chap, was standing stoically next to Lord Packenham, ready to assist with jars, tweezers, and whatnot.

Poppy watched Leopold with the cold detachment of a Spartan mother, observing her newborn offspring for signs of frailty.

"I'm sure he's doing quite alright," I said and took a sip of lemonade. "Where else is the Royal Society going to find another such willing member? Plus, one of them is bound to have a heat stroke, and they will need a new member to top up the Society's coffers."

I didn't vocalize it, but my money was on Lord Mantelbury not making it through the afternoon. His private secretary, Alistair, was a close second.

Poppy kicked at a bright green crawling specimen that looked particularly valuable. I could see that she wrestled with her conscience whether to let Leopold know about it. But as a true sportswoman, she knew the value of sportsmanship and buried the beetle with the toe of her shoe in a bit of sand.

Sitting on my other side was Mr. Lowell. It had

transpired that he was an old friend of James', which explained James' enigmatic reaction to him upon our arrival in Luxor.

As Mr. Lowell had been superseded by the Egyptian police in dealing with Mr. Hargrave's death, he had been free to come to the dung beetle outing with us. And though the Egyptian police had taken over, Mr. Lowell had decided to remain in the area, to protect the interests of British subjects. I appreciated his company, because he was in a position to provide valuable information about how the authorities were proceeding with the case of Mr. Hargrave's death.

"Are more British officials planning to come down from Cairo?" I asked Mr. Lowell.

"It's highly unlikely, at the moment," he replied. "There is nothing to suggest that the deaths of either Lord Chatfield or his brother were anything but the most unfortunate accidents. However, one interesting piece of news made its way to me this morning. The examination of Mr. Hargrave's body by the local doctor revealed a red line, an abrasion around his neck."

I cocked an eyebrow in his direction. "Do you mean he was strangled before the stone fell on his head?"

"No, the injury seems to be more consistent with something like a cord being pulled off his neck," he said.

The mention of a cord jogged my memory. "I

saw Mr. Hargrave wearing an amulet around his neck," I said, "the day I met him at the Egyptian Museum."

Mr. Lowell sat up in his chair, intrigued. "What kind of amulet?"

"I've seen it on the walls of many of the tombs we've visited," I said. "It looks like outstretched wings."

"The Winged Sun of Thebes," Mr. Lowell said, almost to himself.

"What is it?"

"It's an ancient Egyptian symbol associated with royalty, alluding to their divinity," he answered. "But since then, it has taken on many other meanings—it was used by alchemists in the Middle Ages to represent enlightenment, and then by various secret societies."

"Do you think Mr. Hargrave could have been killed for it?" I asked, my mind jumping to Mr. Dalton and his talk of alchemy, eternal life, and the purported secret concealed in the temple.

"I can't say, without having seen it," Mr. Lowell said. "But I should not think so. There are many such amulets about. They were placed inside the bandages of the mummies of members of the royal families. Unless the material it was made out of was particularly valuable, I can't see why it would be of interest to anyone. But even then, who would kill for such a thing? Can you describe it?"

"I saw it only once, but it seemed to be made out

of stone and was no bigger than my palm," I said.

We remained silent for a few moments. The missing medallion added a new layer of mystery to this whole affair. Had Mr. Dalton stolen it? Was it somehow connected to the temple?

"But I'll tell you another thing," Mr. Lowell interrupted my thoughts, "I don't buy that theory of the stone falling off the column and killing Mr. Hargrave."

"What do you mean?" I asked, quite intrigued.

"The wound on Mr. Hargrave's head appeared to be inconsistent with it. If the rock had fallen from the top of the column, the gash on his head would have been deeper. So it might yet turn out that foul play was involved in his death, I'm afraid. I haven't said anything to the Egyptian authorities, so we should keep this between ourselves."

I nodded. The case of Mr. Hargrave's death was becoming quite interesting.

"So you mean someone hit Mr. Hargrave with the rock?" I asked and tried to think back to the temple and Mr. Hargrave's body. "Do you think a woman might have done it?"

He nodded. "Yes. Why do you ask?"

I shrugged my shoulders. "No reason."

I hadn't decided if I should let Mr. Lowell know about what I had overheard Mrs. Gladstone say. The poor woman had to deal with her husband's death. For a moment, I wondered, uncharitably, if she had been predicting Mr. Gladstone's death all along. Had she been anticipating it? But judging by her reaction, the death had come as quite a shock to her.

"Lady Caroline," Mr. Lowell said, drawing me out of my thoughts again. "I have to admit that I am aware of your penchant for mysteries. James mentioned it. I would be grateful to know any thoughts you might have on this matter. There are too many deaths, occurring in too quick a succession, for my liking."

I considered Mr. Lowell for a moment. James had a rather favorable opinion of him. But even James was not quite certain of the nature of Mr. Lowell's capacity in Egypt.

"What strikes me as odd is that many of the people on our boat, excepting the Royal Society, seem to have a motive for wanting the brothers dead," I said. I'd decided to discuss the publicly known details of the case with him and keep the more esoteric occurrences, like my uncle's fez matching the walls of the temple, and the rifling of my uncle's room, private for the time being. "Why were they all traveling together on a Cook and Son tourist cruise?"

"Yes," Mr. Lowell nodded. "An interesting question to consider. Speaking of motives, if there is foul play involved, I would say Mr. Kershaw is the most likely suspect. Do you know his history?"

"His daughter mentioned something about losing a dig concession. And I gathered the dig in question was Mr. Hargrave's site. But I don't know much else. Apparently, his temper gets the better of him."

"Mr. Kershaw's tale of woe is from before my time in Egypt," Mr. Lowell said. "But I telephoned Cairo to get more information on the passengers of your boat from my various friends and contacts, just to know who I was dealing with here." He adjusted himself in his seat. Had he perhaps revealed too much about his mission in Egypt? "Mr. Kershaw is a very capable Egyptologist, by all accounts. But that doesn't get you dig concessions these days. The British have to compete with the Americans. And the Italians are rather good at finding things as well. And even the French still control quite a few sites. So, personality plays an important role in being granted excavation rights by the Department of Antiquities."

"And Mr. Kershaw is too blunt to be loved?" I suggested.

"Yes, apparently he suffers no fools," Mr. Lowell said and laughed. "He tells people their mistakes and gets into arguments over the most trifling points of ancient Egyptian history. So even the Department of Antiquities stays away from him, despite his unquestionable skill."

"What about his history with Lord Chatfield and his brother?"

"Yes, that part is a bit messy, and I'm not certain who is to blame. Mr. Kershaw was the original concession holder of the dig in question. And he blamed the brothers for having the Department of Antiquities take it away from him. But the brothers themselves bore no responsibility for that act. Mr. Kershaw had simply argued with the wrong man, the director of the Egyptian Museum, who retaliated by calling in a few favors. The brothers were simply the next people to get the concession. Also, it's interesting to note, that at the time when Mr. Kershaw lost the dig, it was one of the less desirable places to excavate. It was not a pharaoh's tomb, so there was no great treasure to be found."

"So then it was when the brothers discovered the curse and the myth of treasure that the dig became highly desirable?"

He nodded. "Yes, the brothers traveled to Cairo to let everyone know. And that, apparently, upset Mr. Kershaw even more. There was a shouting match at the Department of Antiquities."

"Do you think he stands a chance of getting the dig now?" I asked.

"The temple your group happened upon has made the dig immensely valuable overnight," Mr. Lowell said. "The Egyptians are bound to be rather fastidious about who they give it to, especially if there is a treasure in it."

"I can't help but think that the discovery of the temple precipitated Mr. Hargrave's death," I said.

"I believe you might be right," he said.

"There is also Mr. Dalton," I said. "He has been quite frank about his interest in the temple. And his interest is not purely scholarly."

"Yes, Mr. Dalton is known for his shady dealings. He tends to pay locals to smuggle antiques out of digs. It's quite prevalent, and he's not the only one doing it. But he does know his stuff and has friends in high places."

"What about Mrs. Gladstone?" I asked. I was still unclear about her role in the deaths. "She seems rather odd. I can't figure out how she predicted the deaths. Does that make her the culprit? Have you found out anything more about her?"

A curious smile spread across Mr. Lowell's handsome features. "Funny you should ask about her," he said, his voice laced with delight. "Mr. Hargrave had sent a message inquiring about her identity to the officials in Cairo."

CHAPTER 22

"Why would Mr. Hargrave enquire about Mrs. Gladstone's identity?" I asked, confused.

"Well, he did not elaborate when he sent the cable from the boat to Cairo," Mr. Lowell said. "Apparently, he was looking for a confirmation of her identity."

"How strange," I said, and cast my thoughts back to our time on the boat. "Did he suspect something about her? I didn't get the impression that they knew each other. She was quite wrong to hold that seance right after Lord Chatfield's death, of course. Her performance was ghastly. I wonder if he suspected her of being a charlatan type of medium?"

Mr. Lowell smirked. "Is there any other kind?"

His observation made me smile. "I suppose not." Though my aunts would probably disagree.

"However, I checked the dates," Mr. Lowell continued. "I compared the date of Mr. Hargrave's communication to Cairo with the date of the seance. The inquiry into her identity was sent a few days before the seance. Almost immediately after the boat departed."

"So it was not the seance that prompted his inquiry," I said. That fact was even more intriguing.

Mr. Lowell nodded. "Exactly. Then what had troubled him about her? I was hoping you would have some insider information, as it were."

I sighed and tried to think back. Nothing about the interactions between the two had been in any way suspicious. "I only noticed a falling out between them after the seance. But what came out of his inquiry? Were the authorities able to find out anything suspicious about Mrs. Gladstone?"

"Unfortunately, she appears to be exactly who she claims to be: a New Yorker, married to a financier. She's known to have a strong interest in the occult, and attends weekly seances in the Gas House District—not a wholesome place to visit, by all accounts. And according to acquaintances, she had developed an interest in the Egyptian occult recently, which prompted her to visit the country. So we still can't account as to why Mr. Hargrave was interested in her identity."

We sat in silence for a few moments, each lost in thought. I glanced at Poppy, who had been sitting unnaturally quiet by my side. In between appraising looks at Leopold, she studied the thick red volume resting in her lap. Now a member of the aristocracy, Poppy had taken it upon herself to explore its intricate web of relations, outlined so succinctly and impenetrably in the *Debrett's Peerage & Baronetage*. I knew only one person who derived pleasure from reading *Debrett's*, and that was my aunt Myrtle, who diligently sent letters to the editors with corrections after each new edition came out.

"Though, it is possible that they had met in New York," Mr. Lowell said.

I turned my attention back to him. "Mr. Hargrave had visited New York?" I said. "Did Mrs. Babcock go with him?"

"No, why do you ask?"

"There was a friendship that developed between the two women on the boat. The attraction they felt for each other would be more easily explained if they had met before. Plus, I thought it rather odd that Mrs. Babcock was so quick to give Mrs. Gladstone an alibi for the time of Mr. Hargrave's death."

"Ah, you noticed that as well?" Mr. Lowell said.

"Yes, I wondered if Mrs. Babcock had not been attempting to provide an alibi for herself," I said. "But I wonder what her motive could be."

"By all indications, Mrs. Babcock had excellent relations with her employer and even with Lord Chatfield."

"Could they have had a falling out over the discovery of the temple? Could she have killed Mr. Hargrave in the heat of the moment? But if that were so, what would make her act so suddenly?"

"I will look into any motivation she may have had to do away with her employer. The Egyptologist community is quite small and news travels quickly. Incidentally, she has already approached another archeologist to be his secretary. And has even spoken to Mr. Kershaw for a possible partnership, if he can secure the vacant dig."

A vague thought formed in my mind. Perhaps Mrs. Babcock and Mr. Kershaw had worked this scheme together in order to secure rights over the dig. I thought back to the underground temple, but besides overhearing Mrs. Gladstone's unexpected utterance to her companion, I had not observed anything else strange. I wondered what Mr. Lowell would make of Mrs. Gladstone's declaration.

"Perhaps I forgot to mention it," I said casually, "but I overheard the strangest conversation between Mrs. Gladstone and Miss Parker as I was making my way out of the temple. Mrs. Gladstone remarked that the wrong person had died. I initially thought that she might be confessing to killing the wrong person—"

"And you didn't think to share this with me?" Mr. Lowell said in mock reprimand.

I shrugged and smiled. "Now I wonder if she had been predicting her husband's death instead all this time? Could she have been expecting it? How did her husband die, by the way? Was he ill?"

"Not ill. He fell down the stairs at his home."

"Any suggestion of foul play? Was he perhaps pushed? Did the servants see anything?" I asked. The servants always knew.

Mr. Lowell shook his head. "It's the most unlucky coincidence. Mr. Gladstone was something of a miser and, with his wife away, he placed the servants on furlough, citing a lack of things for them to do while his wife was away. So he was all alone when he tripped down the stairs and died."

"Who found him?"

"A policeman was sent round to check on him after he failed to turn up for work and was not answering the telephone. Apparently, he missed a rather important meeting."

"Could one of the servants have snuck back into the house and pushed him?"

"We'll have to wait and see what the newspapers tell us," Mr. Lowell said.

"Poor Mrs. Gladstone," I said. Though I did not particularly like the woman, it was a rather unpleasant way to end a holiday. "Though, it does seem like the spirits warned her of his death." *That should give her some comfort*, I thought, unkindly.

"Well, at least it's clear that she didn't push him down the stairs," Mr. Lowell said and smirked.

"Have we misjudged her? She couldn't perhaps be some powerful mystic who is able to predict and influence death?" I suggested, though I didn't believe it myself. Yet, here in Egypt, magic seemed almost possible.

Mr. Lowell gave me a dubious glance.

"If all this time Mrs. Gladstone has been predicting her husband's death, does that then absolve her of Mr. Hargrave's?" I said, thinking aloud.

Mr. Lowell did not answer.

I wondered if my original suspicion, that she had killed Mr. Hargrave by mistake, still held. How could we be positive that she had left for Alexandria? What if she came back here to kill the person she had meant to all along?

I turned to Mr. Lowell. "Perhaps the authorities should make certain that Mrs. Gladstone and Miss Parker make it onto their boat for New York."

Mr. Lowell sent me another skeptical glance, but nodded.

Any further discussion was cut short by the summons to lunch.

Lunch accommodations in the desert were very much in the style of a safari: tents, folding chairs and folding tables. Thus, the members of the younger generation—Poppy, Leo, James and I, Mr. Lowell, vile Hector and a few other private secretaries, who didn't matter much—were sitting at a table separate from the Lords.

All this talk of Mrs. Gladstone had jogged my mind to an interaction I had observed between Miss Parker and Alistair on the day we had boarded our boat. I had meant to ask him about it, but never got the chance.

"Alistair," I said, turning to him, "how do you happen to know Miss Parker?"

He blushed violently. "I can't say that I know her," he stammered. Vile Hector let out a whistle and Alistair looked almost ready to give up. "I met her at the Cook and Son office in Cairo," he persevered.

"Indeed?" I said. "What was she doing?"

"She came in after me, and was rather confused about the whole process of acquiring a passage up the Nile. I helped her work through the choices. Though, as it turned out, ours was one of the only boats that had any space left on it..." He faltered, perhaps thinking back to the Lords' displeasure of having to share a boat with the plebeians.

"So the reason Mrs. Gladstone was on our boat was you?"

Alistair looked uncertain about whether that was some sort of reprimand and just blushed again. But I had not meant it as such. All I was attempting to discern was whether Mrs. Gladstone's presence on our boat had been accidental.

"When I was leaving the ticket agency," Alistair ventured again, "Miss Parker seemed particularly interested to learn from the agent which boats were carrying Americans. So I was rather surprised to see her on our boat the morning of our departure."

"Yes, indeed. That is most interesting." Why had Miss Parker and her employer ended up on a boat with almost no Americans?

"I was perhaps a bit rash in my presumption to have made her acquaintance at the ticket office," he continued, "and acted rather impetuously in approaching her on the bridge."

Poor Alistair. How was he to ever get a girl if he was still harping on about the event on the bridge?

Lunch continued in silence. I was lost in my thoughts about the enigma that was Mrs. Gladstone.

"You know what I think?" Alistair began tentatively. "I think..." He gave up.

"Yes?" I encouraged him.

"I think she was quite beastly to the boat staff," he finally coughed out. He looked around sheepishly, as though waiting to see if anyone would throw up an objection to his observation.

"Who was, Alistair?" I said and cast a quick glance at Poppy.

"Mrs. Gladstone. It was as though she'd never had staff before."

"What makes you say that?" I asked, intrigued.

"Well, there was something very common about the way she treated them. She was rude to them."

I nodded. I'd noticed the same thing. I glanced at Poppy again, who was tucking happily into her pudding. While Poppy was overbearing in her manner to the staff, it was only because she reveled in taking charge and usually assumed that people were going about things the wrong way. Mrs. Gladstone's conduct towards the staff had been quite different. She had been just plain rude.

"It was unseemly," Alistair added, encouraged by my nod. "It reminded me of a chum from school. His parents were new money. I visited them once during the summer holidays, and they spoke to their staff, as though superior to them...Mrs. Gladstone's behavior on the boat quite reminded me of them..."

"Bravo, Alistair," I said. It really had been quite an astute observation.

"You should not encourage him," James said to me later on that afternoon.

"What do you mean?"

"I mean that you should not lead Alistair on and raise his hopes," James said gently.

"I do not do that," I objected.

"I know you don't mean to, old bean. But all the same, he doesn't know about us, and I can see the way he looks at you whenever you pay him a compliment."

I sighed. What was it about weak men? Why did they always pin their hopes on the most unattainable of women? I felt as though, ever since my debut, my life had been one long flight from such men—Alistair, Cecil, even dear Leopold.

"Perhaps we should tell everyone of our plans," James suggested, referring to our unofficial understanding.

"Not now," I objected. "We have not even told our parents. And we can't tell them with a telegram from Egypt." I gave him a peck on the cheek to soften the blow.

He nodded. I wondered how much longer he would be so understanding. Originally, we had postponed any official announcement because of Leopold and Poppy's wedding. And now we were in Egypt and away from our families.

But was that the only reason that was stopping me? Would I even be comfortable enough to tell James what was keeping me back? I shook the troublesome thought away.

"Plus, Alistair is harmless," I said, prodding the conversation away from our non-existent engagement. "He has so little going for him at the moment, with Miss Parker on her way to America. And if even Alistair noticed that there was something untoward about Mrs. Gladstone, she really needs to be investigated further."

CHAPTER 23

Returning to the hotel, I saw Miss Kershaw on the verandah by herself and ventured to join her. She had been absent from the public areas of the hotel, and I hadn't had a chance to speak to her. There was something about her reaction to Mr. Hargrave's death that was bothering me.

"Hello, Miss Kershaw," I said, gliding up to her table.

My greeting evidently startled her. She had been gazing over the river, as though lost in thought. At the sound of my voice, she jumped and quickly slid into the pocket of her trousers, something she had been holding in her hands.

I caught only its edge with my eyes, but it was enough to make me question everything I had thought of Miss Kershaw up to now. I frowned and wondered how to proceed.

"Oh, hello, Lady Caroline," she said, endeavoring to make her voice sunny and relaxed.

"May I join you?"

"Of course." She gestured to the other chair at the table.

"I'm glad to see you are doing a little better," I said.

"I am, thank you." But the dullness in her eyes told a different story.

We sat in silence as I fumbled for a while over which point to address first.

"Do you know who will be taking over the Temple of Khepri dig now?" I said, approaching the subject from as far away as possible, hoping it would lead me to the answers I was seeking.

"A decision hasn't been made by the Department of Antiquities quite yet. My father is hoping it will be him, but I'm not so certain."

"I hear the archaeological community of Egypt is rather small. With Mr. Hargrave and his brother gone, your father stands a better chance."

"What are you suggesting, Lady Caroline?" Miss Kershaw asked, suddenly tense.

I reprimanded myself mentally for phrasing it quite like that. "I'm sorry, Miss Kershaw, that came out wrong," I said, trying to appease her and hoping that she would not clam up or leave just yet. "All I meant was that if all other teams are busy on other sites, the Department of Antiquities might turn to your father, whatever their past disagreements might have been. He seems like quite a knowledgeable man."

Miss Kershaw nodded.

"Is the dig something you perhaps would be interested in taking over?" I asked, cautiously.

"Ha! A mere woman?!" Some of the fire returned to her bright blue eyes. "Even in Britain that would be unheard of, let alone Egypt."

I nodded. I understood.

"The Tomb of Ahmose and the Temple of Khepri do present a rather interesting opportunity for new research," she continued. "I had hoped to do more work alongside Mr. Hargrave...He didn't hold any antiquated attitudes towards women and their place in Egyptology. Or society..." She hesitated, and I saw my chance to ask her more about Mr. Hargrave.

"Yes, Mr. Hargrave seemed like a nice man. I think his accident has affected you quite deeply," I said gently.

She nodded, but did not elaborate.

I wondered about the best way to bring up her reaction to Mr. Hargrave's death, which had both perplexed me and had made me wonder about their true relationship.

"Lady Caroline," she said after a few moments of silence, "may I tell you something I have told no one else?"

My heart skipped a beat, but I tried to keep my face calm. I smiled pleasantly at her.

"I'm only telling you this because I know you are a good egg. I quite enjoy the rather amusing and madcap predicaments you seem to get into, according to the society pages." She smiled at me and her eyes sparkled.

I really liked Miss Kershaw, and I hoped she would also turn out to be a good egg. But the item she had hidden in her pocket left me with a nagging doubt.

"What is it, Miss Kershaw?"

"I haven't told anyone, and I hope this information will not make its way to my father, but I think you would understand, since I suspect you have a secret attachment to James." She looked at me rather conspiratorially. "Nigel, Mr. Hargrave, and I were secretly engaged."

I nodded. I had suspected an attachment between the two. Poor Miss Parker, I thought. She never stood a chance. And then a rather disturbing thought popped into my mind—what if Miss Parker had discovered the secret engagement and bludgeoned Mr. Hargrave to death in anger? I shook the disturbing thought away.

"Why keep it secret?" I asked.

"It happened while I was in New York, studying. Mr. Hargrave visited my advisor for some reason, some sort of research. And our relationship blossomed from there."

"But why didn't you tell anyone?"

"I was afraid of how my father would react, I suppose. Given my father's animosity towards Nigel and his brother."

I nodded. "So, you weren't on our boat by chance?" I said.

She shook her head, and her wild hair bounced.

"No. I knew Nigel was going to be on that boat. I hoped that if my father could get to know him better, he would discover what a wonderful man he was."

"And would allow you to marry Mr. Hargrave," I said.

She nodded as sorrow transformed her pretty face. My heart went out to her.

"Are you not worried that the authorities would find out?" I asked. They were still puzzling over Mr. Hargrave's death and had not given up the foul play theory. "They might think it suspicious that you kept that information from them."

"How would they find out? No one knew."

"Perhaps he confided in a friend?"

"He didn't have many of those. Not close ones, anyway. Something about competition for dig concessions pits archeologists in Egypt against each other. Even if he did confide in a friend, it is nothing to be ashamed of. We only kept it secret because of my father. If the authorities find out, I have nothing to hide."

I looked at her pocket. She noticed my glance and pulled out the item I had seen her hide away. She ran her thumb over its outline.

"Miss Kershaw, unless there are two of these winged amulets on a leather strap, I believe this one belonged to Mr. Hargrave."

She nodded. "How did you know?"

"I saw him wearing it on the day we first met at the Egyptian Museum. He was less formally dressed, and the amulet hung around his neck. May I ask how you got it?"

Her eyes filled with tears. "I'm ashamed to say that I took it off his neck when I found him." She looked down at her now trembling hands. "I knew he was dead. And a fear that I had nothing of his overtook me. I wanted to keep a memento..."

"So you ripped it off his neck," I said, rather puzzled by the violent act.

"I heard people coming, and I panicked. There was no time to remove it gently from around his neck. I didn't want anyone to see me. What would they think of me? I knew it was my only chance. I couldn't hope to reason with the Egyptian authorities to let me keep it."

That explained the red mark around Mr. Hargrave's neck.

"Did anyone see you do it?"

"No," she said, shaking her head. "By the time the two women came, I had put it away in my pocket."

"Is it valuable?" I asked, but I knew that was not the reason Miss Kershaw had taken it.

"No. Its value is only sentimental. It was Nigel's first real archeological find. He'd discovered it working alongside his father, when he was a boy. He loved it."

"So that explains away the only clue that

suggested foul play," I said. I wondered whether I would tell Mr. Lowell about it. But as Miss Kershaw seemed to have lost enough, I didn't want to add to her troubles. Though how the police would explain the red mark on his neck was a mystery to me. "I guess we have to conclude that Mr. Hargrave's death was an accident, after all."

"I would not be so sure," Miss Kershaw said.

"Why?" Her statement surprised me.

"The evening of the seance, after it was done, I followed Nigel out of the lounge. I wanted to talk to him, and be of comfort to him. That preposterous woman had no right to pretend to summon his brother's ghost in such an absurd manner. It was all quite atrocious."

I nodded in agreement.

"I could not find him at first," she continued. "But I then happened upon him and Mrs. Gladstone quite unexpectedly, in a dark corner of the deck. The conversation was at its conclusion, but it sounded to me as though Nigel was accusing the woman of being a fraud."

So he had actually confronted her about his suspicions, I mused. That was an intriguing piece of information that presented new possibilities about Mr. Hargrave's death.

"How did she react?" I asked.

"She laughed it off," Miss Kershaw said. "She said something about having met her only once, and how could he presume to know her well?"

"Oh, so they had met before?!"

"Yes. Or at least Nigel thought so. I asked him about it later, and he said that he was sure they had met before. Something was off about her, but he couldn't say exactly what."

"Where had they met?"

"Mrs. Gladstone had come to the university in New York, while he was there, to ask something about Egyptology. And he remembered her, because she had asked about Egyptian cats."

"That does sound rather *like* Mrs. Gladstone," I said hesitantly.

Miss Kershaw nodded. "That was the trouble. After their conversation, he began doubting himself. He thought he had made a mistake. He felt terrible. But he was still angry about the seance."

"Yes," I said, thinking aloud. "It's clear that he was suspicious of her. But why? He had sent an inquiry about her to Cairo from the boat, did you know?" I said.

"No." She shook her head. "And have the authorities looked into Mrs. Gladstone's identity?" Miss Kershaw asked eagerly. "Is she who she says she is?"

"Yes, they have," I said. "They didn't find anything untoward, I'm afraid. But this altercation between them is rather suggestive."

"Do you think she may have had something to do with Nigel's death?" Miss Kershaw asked with trepidation. "She predicted his death. And then there was the mummy. It all seems to point to her."

I sighed. "I don't know." I didn't know what to think. Was Mrs. Gladstone responsible for Mr. Hargrave's death, or her husband's death, or both, or neither? Things felt out of order. She had predicted the death before Mr. Hargrave had confronted her on the deck. I was not certain that she'd had his death in mind during the seance.

"But if Mrs. Gladstone is somehow involved," Miss Kershaw pressed on, "we have to let the authorities know. I've seen you in the company of Mr. Lowell. He seems like a decent chap. Maybe you can ask him to look into it." Miss Kershaw was almost pleading.

"Yes, of course. And if she is involved, the authorities have plenty of time to catch her. She'll be cloistered onto a cross-Atlantic steamer soon, so she can't get away easily now."

Miss Kershaw then left me to change for dinner. I remained on the verandah, wondering if she had been truthful with me. She would not have been the first woman to lie to me about engagements and such. And was her explanation about the winged amulet accurate? What if it had some significance connected to the temple and its treasure? But I chose to believe her, although that might have been partly because of her compliments about my exploits in the society pages.

And another thing, if Miss Kershaw and her

father had not been on our boat quite by accident, I wondered if anyone else had been on the boat by design? Mrs. Gladstone? Mr. Dalton?

However, it was the revelation about the conversation between Mrs. Gladstone and Mr. Hargrave that had me most intrigued. What had it been about Mrs. Gladstone that had prompted Mr. Hargrave to enquire about her even before she'd held her seance? And what was it about the seance that made him accuse her of being a fraud?

I left the verandah to find out.

CHAPTER 24

The sun was setting over the Nile and its rays glittered atop the water's surface like thousands of coins. The golden light bathed the ancient ruins on the banks in a soft glow. A warm breeze fanned the leaves of the palm trees along the banks, and played gently on our faces. One could surely envy the ancient pharaohs and their eternal resting places along the river's shores.

I was sitting by James' side on the open deck of Poppy's dahabiya, sipping cocktails and awaiting dinner, prepared by the boat's chef. I looked forward to an evening away from the Royal Society, spent only in the company of close friends.

We sat moored to the river's shore, the languid waters of the Nile flowing past us. As we sipped our cocktails, the boat rocked gently. I watched the blue sky turn from pink to purple. Sundown was a magical time on the Nile.

"If the Elysian fields were a river, they would be the Nile," I said to the breeze.

Surrounded by these ancient monuments, it was easy to dismiss the problems of the present and surrender oneself to eternity. I slipped into a comfortable oblivion induced by the pre-dinner drinks. But even as I was lulled into forgetfulness, the deaths we had encountered on this trip were not far from my mind. That death was one's constant companion, and that life was brutish and short, was never so evident as in Egypt—the stray dogs, the begging children, the poverty, the dust, the unrelenting desert sands.

"I have to say," Poppy declared, breaking into my thoughts, "I had begun to worry that I had made the wrong decision coming to Egypt for our honeymoon. I feared it was all rather dull—all sphinxes, sand, and dates. But it's turned out to be treasure and curses! How exciting!"

"Surely, you can't think there is a curse?" James objected.

"But why not?" Poppy protested. "What about all these deaths?"

"Yes, it's rather difficult to think that all of them are coincidental," I conceded.

"How many is it now?" Poppy asked, taking a bite of some sort of sugary fried balls the dahabiya chef had prepared for us. They were rather good. She passed one to Leopold, who was sitting by her side, with a blanket across his knees. He hung on Poppy's every word, but did not dare contribute to the conversation. Though he probably would not have been able to, even if he'd wanted to, as Poppy kept filling his mouth with sticky pastries.

The table in front of us was laden with all sorts of desserts to go with our cocktails, of which I only recognized the small squares that looked like baklava. The influence of the Ottoman empire was quite apparent in the food.

"Four," I said, drawing my attention back to the deaths.

"Four? Who is the fourth?" asked James.

"The uncle who died in England was the first," I said, reminding him of the death that had occurred just before we had set off on our trip up the Nile.

"You're counting him?" James countered.

"Why not?" I shrugged. "The newspapers thought his death was connected to the curse."

"Surely his death was a coincidence," he said.

"But we should still count it as part of the curse," Poppy said. "It occurred right after the brothers opened the cursed tomb, according to the newspapers."

I nodded. "Next came Lord Chatfield's death," I said.

"Which was an accident," James added.

"And now his body has been recovered," Poppy interjected. News that Lord Chatfield's body had washed up on the shore of a small village along the Nile had reached us just before dinner.

"And after that, his brother died," Poppy continued.

"Out of all these deaths, Mr. Hargrave's is the only death that could have been planned," I said.

"But how? He died in a temple that had been just discovered," Poppy objected.

"Yes, if he was murdered, his murder was definitely opportunistic," I agreed. "But the killer could have been planning to bump off Mr. Hargrave for a while and just used the opportunity presented by a dark temple and plentiful rocks."

"And we've established that quite a few people on the boat could have wanted him dead, especially after the temple was discovered," James added. I had shared with him my thoughts on various people's motives for wanting Mr. Hargrave dead. "But who's the fourth death?"

"Mrs. Gladstone's husband in New York, of course!" I exclaimed.

"Surely that death cannot be connected to any of the deaths here," James protested.

"But Gassy's right," Poppy jumped in. "His death has to count towards the curse. Mrs. Gladstone was part of the party that went inside the temple—" Poppy gave me a curious sideways glance, but did not elaborate on the thought that troubled her.

"And yet, Mr. Gladstone's death is the only one that is not in the Hargrave family," I said. "Why?"

"It's the curse," Poppy said again, sounding very much like Mrs. Gladstone. But I knew she was saying it in jest.

"Perhaps," I said. "But it's hard to envisage so

many deaths without suspecting that someone had a hand in at least some of them. And I don't mean a power from the beyond."

While I was only humoring Poppy about the curse, I was certain that there was a connection between the deaths. Why would four men die in succession? I needed to discover what that connection was.

The announcement of dinner turned our thoughts to the exotic and delicious dishes being served in front of us, and the deaths were not discussed further. But the cloak of night that had enveloped us by the end of dinner turned my thoughts towards the secret temple again.

While I had dismissed the curse, I was still fascinated by the notion that the temple might hide treasure. The lining of Uncle's fez suggested that particular part of the legend, at least, might be true. But as no one had tried to pinch Uncle Albert's fez a second time, and as the fez-maker's nephew had not contacted us again, it was time to bring the fez lining to the temple, and see what events it might set in motion.

Leopold was now busy counting his beetles for the competition under a bright lantern (attracting quite a few moths), and when Poppy went below deck to torment the crew over some type of boating knot or other, I saw my chance to speak to James privately.

"James, what does your friend, Mr. Lowell, do

here in Egypt?" I asked.

"Old Ratty? Not entirely sure, old bean," he said. "Something to do with the British government and its interests." He shrugged. "Hadn't seen him in years until running across him here. Rather a sad story, his. Lost both of his parents. Some distant uncle or other paid his school fees. Was supposed to come into a bit of money when the uncle died. Sorry, what did you want to know about him?"

"Is he a spy?" I said, lifting an eyebrow.

James laughed and his eyes sparkled with the lights strung across the deck. During the time we'd been in Egypt, his fair hair had grown lighter under the onslaught of the sun, and his skin had taken on the shade of someone just returned from the French Riviera.

"What makes you say that?" he asked, bringing my thoughts back to the matter at hand.

"Mr. Lowell strikes me as a person with many connections," I said. "He doesn't seem to have an official title or post here in Egypt, and yet, even the Egyptian officials seem to be wary around him, and give him the information he needs without resistance."

James nodded. "Well spotted. I'm sure there is some truth to that. But he hasn't told even me what he's up to here."

"Perhaps adding another argument for my secret agent theory," I said.

He simply smiled. "Why are you so interested

in him?" he asked after a few moments, with a mischievous twinkle in his eye. "Should I be worried?"

I blushed. "No, nothing like that," I said. "It's about Uncle Albert's fez."

James's laugh rang out into the dark night. "I'd quite forgotten about it. What has happened to Lord Tatham's fez that requires the involvement of the Foreign Office?" he asked, bemusement coloring his voice. "Don't tell me you've received another note from the fez-maker's nephew?"

I shook my head. I rather wished I had received another communication from him, especially now that the temple he had seemed to anticipate had been located. What was the point of the fez? What did it all mean?

"No, listen. It's rather serious," I said, lowering my voice. "It sounds rather extraordinary, but the walls of that temple were covered in the same golden scarabs as the lining of Uncle Albert's fez."

"Some sort of local motif, I would imagine," James said.

"That's what I thought, but there is more to it. Uncle Albert said that someone had rifled through his cabin on the boat."

Having lounged in a rather relaxed manner until now, James sat up. "What? Why didn't you say something about it sooner?"

"I only found out about it recently myself. Uncle Albert didn't want to worry me."

"Who could have done this? One of the staff?"

I shrugged. "Or one of the passengers," I suggested.

"Was anything taken? Don't tell me someone took his fez!"

"No, nothing of the sort. It appears that nothing was taken. But it is rather strange, don't you agree? Uncle Albert, of course, is convinced that whoever searched his room was looking for his fez."

James rolled his eyes. "But they didn't take the fez."

"No, but that's probably only because Wilford had cut the lining out of it—long story," I said, answering James' questioning look.

"And you think whoever it was, was looking for the secret message hidden in the lining?" James said, but still sounding unconvinced. "Why didn't they take the lining?"

"Well, Wilford had hidden it quite expertly," I said and smiled.

"Where?"

"Inside Uncle Albert's large carpet," I said and laughed. "As there was no way to unroll the carpet on the boat, the fez lining made it quite safe to Luxor. But who knows if and when the thieves will try again."

James threw me a dubious look, but did not contradict me.

"And then there is also the man with the scar," I

added.

That got James' attention. "What man?"

"An Egyptian. The first time I saw him was at the market, when Uncle Albert went to the fez-maker. He was standing to the side, observing us. Looking quite menacing. I think he followed us out of the market, but I can't be certain. The nephew turned around a few times, as though worried someone was after us. And then I saw him again as our boat was departing Cairo. He was on the quay and he nodded to someone on the boat."

"Did you see who?"

I shrugged.

"Why didn't you say something before?" James asked with concern.

"I didn't take any of it seriously. Not until I saw the walls of the temple and Uncle told me about the break-in."

James nodded. "So what do you want old Ratty to do?"

I crinkled my nose at the ugly sobriquet bestowed on the handsome Mr. Lowell, but now was not the time to ask about it. "I want to go down into the temple again. I want to explore it, now that Wilford has retrieved the lining out of the rug."

James nodded. "I'll see what I can do about it. But I don't think that would be possible, especially not with the guards they have stationed at the entrance now."

CHAPTER 25

Mr. Lowell's connections in Egypt, however, indeed ran deep. Word came the next morning that all was set for our expedition.

"How did he manage to secure us permission to enter?" I asked James, fascinated by the extent of his friend's web of influence. We were walking in a secluded part of the hotel's gardens. There were few places where two people who were not officially engaged could meet in private, without arousing suspicion or outrage.

We made certain no one was about before continuing our conversation. And in any case, if anyone tried to sneak up on us, they were bound to get tangled in the insect nets the Royal Society had extended across every pathway in this part of the garden.

"Well, the thing is, our outing doesn't seem to be quite above board," James said.

"What do you mean?"

"Old Ratty didn't elaborate, but we are to enter under the cover of darkness when the guards are undertaking their evening prayers. He tells me they are likely to abandon their posts in order to fulfill their religious obligation. He's secured a boat to ferry us across the river. We'll have to be fairly quick and stealthy about it."

"That might be an issue. I don't think those are Uncle Albert's strengths," I objected.

"Caroline, you can't be serious!" James cried out. "Your uncle is not the person to bring on this expedition," he said in a much quieter tone.

"We can't leave him out," I said, quite firmly. My mind was made up on the matter. "It's his fez. The fez-maker entrusted it to him. If anyone has the right to go down into the temple and look for its secrets, it's Uncle Albert. We'll have to find a way to have him come along. He'll be quite alright once inside the temple. It's getting him there, without drawing too much suspicion, that will present a challenge."

In the end, we decided that trying to have Uncle Albert act with any semblance of secrecy was quite futile and would only draw more attention to us.

So Uncle Albert and I set off in the early afternoon to cross to the west bank under the guise of visiting the Valley of the Kings and having a look at the Tutankhamen tomb. On the way back, we lingered behind, Uncle Albert feigning exhaustion. Or perhaps he was not pretending. Regardless, we dismissed our donkey minders and their animals, saying that we found walking more enjoyable, which was also not far from the truth. But since we paid off the handlers quite handsomely, and as it was nearing dinner time, they did not object.

With the coast clear, we made, rather slowly, for the two hills marking our final destination. Mr. Lowell had reconnoitered the area and left us a picnic basket, in lieu of dinner, behind a large boulder at the base of the southern hill. James had been instructed to let everyone at dinner know that Uncle Albert had suffered a heat stroke and was in his room, with me in attendance. Wilford was to turn any snoopers away.

We thus lay in wait for our co-conspirators. Uncle Albert had brought the folding tooled-leather stool he had acquired at the Cairo market, and now I rather wished I'd purchased one as well. But the sand beneath me felt quite soft and the rock behind my back was quite warm, and we soon relaxed enough to nibble on the rations in our basket.

I only hoped that James and Mr. Lowell would arrive before the scorpions came out of their hiding places for their nightly hunt.

As the sun set behind us, and the last rays disappeared from the walls of the temples in Luxor across the river, the air turned chilly. We wrapped ourselves in the blankets that came with the picnic basket and waited.

The first stars became visible, and soon the whole sky was filled with their twinkling light. I began to worry that James and Mr. Lowell were not coming. Elaborate stories of reasons why they had been delayed weaved themselves unbidden in my mind. I marveled at the calm manner in which Uncle Albert was waiting, but presently discovered that he was slumbering on his stool.

As more time passed, I wondered if perhaps we should return to the hotel. Despite employing some reconnaissance sitting exercises I had learned at Frau Baumgartnerhoff's finishing school—the slightly peculiar Swiss institution I had attended—my bottom had grown numb. I got up to move about and took the opportunity to examine the black waters of the Nile for any movement.

The darkness had brought with it an unnerving silence, as tourists and workers had left the west bank for the comforts of Luxor across the water. The excavated tombs in the surrounding hills gaped with their black mouths. And now other sounds began to emerge—the sounds of animals, one hoped, stirring in the night.

It was with great relief that I heard rhythmic footsteps on the sand. I secretly worried that it might be some sort of desert wild cat and waited until two silhouettes appeared, outlined quite clearly against the lights of Luxor. I breathed a sigh of relief when I discerned James.

"What kept you so long?" I whispered as they came near.

"We're not late," James said. "It's just after the appointed time. But we had to make our way up here without torches, so no one would see us."

"What now?" I asked.

"We move closer to the entrance of the camp and wait for the next prayer call. It shouldn't be long now," Mr. Lowell said.

I'd heard the call at sunset and knew that another call to prayer was to follow after dark. We took our positions at the ingress between the two hills and waited.

As the faint sing-song calls from the minarets in Luxor weaved their way across the water to us, we observed the men left to guard the temple scramble about.

We made our way, keeping to the shadows, proceeding slowly, both to gauge our surroundings and to ensure that Uncle Albert was not blundering about. But the mission seemed to have had a rejuvenating effect on him, and he was quite spritely in his maneuvers.

The camp, now free of any archaeologists or workers, had a ghostly air about it. The tents flapped empty in the cold wind that came down the hills. Most of the camp was in darkness and the few lanterns were gathered near where the guards were performing their rituals.

We stopped to observe the entrance to the temple from a distance. It was covered with canvas.

"That should not be too difficult to deal with," Mr. Lowell whispered. "I'd feared something heavier and more burdensome to shift." Thus encouraged, he motioned for us to follow him.

Getting inside the temple was easier than I had imagined. We slipped under the canvas cover, dashed down the steps, and proceeded as far as we could into the depths of the temple by feeling our way along the walls. We only stopped when we came to a fork in the passageway.

Mr. Lowell was the first to switch on his torch. "It should be safe to have some light now. It should not be visible from the entrance."

"Magnificent," James said, looking at the hieroglyph paintings on the walls and ceiling around him. "Exquisite craftsmanship."

"Which way now?" Mr. Lowell asked, as though unmoved by the marvelous sight. "Did you want to go straight to the chamber where I'd found you, or do you want to explore a bit?"

I hesitated. "Let's explore, and if we don't find anything more interesting, we'll make our way to the hall with the columns." There was no need to rush. We were not likely to get another opportunity to explore this temple.

We set off down the right-hand corridor. Most of the passageways turned out to be dead ends and very few seemed to lead to a chamber. I felt like Mole in *The Wind in the Willows*, following Ratty, exploring Mr. Badger's underground sett.

I smiled at my childish notions. *We were here to find unimaginable treasure*, I reminded myself, and began thinking more along the lines of Scheherazade and Ali Baba.

"This is it!" I exclaimed, when we got to the room Uncle Albert and I had first discovered.

The room was just as awe-inspiring as the first time I had seen it. Golden scarabs littered the blue walls and ceiling like stars in the night sky.

"You're right, it does look exactly like the fez lining," James said. "Lord Tatham, did you bring it?"

My heart skipped. I hoped Uncle Albert had not left it behind. And though he fumbled a bit, and wondered aloud where Wilford might have put it, he finally retrieved it from an inside pocket with a triumphant, "Aha!"

Mr. Lowell held his torch over the silk cloth. We all looked from it to the golden scarabs glinting on the walls. What did it all mean?

"Each scarab seems to have a slightly different design," Uncle Albert said.

We looked again. At first glance, all the scarabs looked the same, they were the same size and the same color. But on closer inspection, each scarab differed from its brethren by the shape of its antennas, or leg position, or wing shape, or the ornamentation of its wings. We ran our fingers over the designs, followed them all around the room, and explored the walls for any hidden openings. But search as we may, we couldn't make out purpose or meaning.

"Shall we go to the hall?" Mr. Lowell suggested. "There are more of these there."

I hesitated. In all the excitement, I'd quite forgotten about Mr. Hargrave's death and his body. Would there still be a blood stain on the ground? A shiver ran down my spine. What if his ghost roamed the corridors? I shook my head. There was nothing to worry about. We were the only ones here.

We weaved our way to where we thought the great hall was. It was rather more difficult to locate it this time in the maze of corridors.

I mused how easy it would have been for Mr. Hargrave's killer, if there was such a person, to have slipped into one of these tunnels and then joined us again after Miss Kershaw had screamed.

"Here it is," Mr. Lowell announced as we entered the great chamber with the columns.

We raised our torches to illuminate its walls and peered into the shadowed vaults of the ceiling. Here, the same golden scarabs, each with its slightly unique design, covered the walls.

But again, look as we may, we could not discern a meaningful pattern. And though the scarabs embroidered on the silk lining were very much like the ones on the walls, they appeared to be arranged in a different pattern.

We examined the stone columns, which

themselves were carved with rings of hieroglyphs. And we inspected the statue of Khepri in the middle of the hall, running our hands over its alabaster human body and gazing up to its smooth basalt beetle head. The plinth of the statue was carved with the same golden scarabs, but the pattern did not match the one on Uncle's silk. We split to examine the walls. And while the rest of us scurried about, Uncle Albert seemed more methodical in his search.

"Over here," Uncle Albert cried out. "It's here!"

CHAPTER 26

James, Mr. Lowell and I ran towards Uncle Albert from different parts of the hall, the light beams of our torches dancing among the columns. What had my uncle discovered?

He was smiling as we approached, his hands behind his back, chest forward, shuffling with enthusiastic energy in one spot. He waited for us to gather around him before turning to the scarabs on the wall behind him.

"This patch on the wall here," he said and pointed to a group of scarabs, "matches the scarabs on the lining." We trained our beams on the spot. "See the curvature of the pronotum on this one?" Uncle Albert continued, "And the striations of the elytra of this one here? No? It's easiest if you follow the carvings on their wings, then."

I looked back and forth between the silk pattern and the pattern on the wall. Indeed, the designs matched down to the last spiral detail on a wing.

Mr. Lowell had not waited for confirmation and had begun running his torch and free hand over the wall, around the perimeter of the pattern. "But how can this be?!" he said. "I cannot perceive any fissures in the wall. I was hoping for a hidden treasure chamber. But perhaps it's only a map of some kind." He strode back and examined the wall from afar.

"Perhaps you have to press this one," Uncle Albert said and stepped forward with confidence. He pushed down on one of the scarabs and it depressed under his fingers.

We waited as a rumbling, grating sound grew louder, and in a moment it became apparent why Mr. Lowell had not been able to detect any grooves in the wall immediately around the scarab pattern. A door, if one could call it that, as tall as doors on cathedrals and about as wide, receded slightly into the wall.

"How did you know which one to press?" Mr. Lowell asked, incredulous, as he stared with hungry eyes at the sunken slab of stone in the wall.

"It was the one that looked like the mark of the fez-maker. It's scattered all around the walls here. But of course, the trick was knowing which one to press. It was the only one that lay inside the matching pattern on the wall," my uncle said.

Mr. Lowell considered the recess for a few more moments and then pushed on it. The slab of stone began to swing inwards, as though on hinges.

James was about to speak when a voice behind us interrupted him.

"So you've found it!"

The American drawl of the speaker was unmistakable. We spun around to find Mr. Dalton standing amongst the columns. And with him was the man with the scar. I frowned.

"What are you doing here, Dalton?" James asked.

"I could ask you the same thing," the American replied. "I knew you were up to something. My friend here has been keeping an eye on the old man," he said and gestured towards my uncle. "When my friend told me that Lord Tatham hadn't returned from the Tutankhamen tomb, I got suspicious. And when I saw you two slip out of the hotel after sunset, I decided to follow. And look what we have here."

He strode forward, and we turned around to stare at the gaping cavern behind us. The door, having swung all the way back, revealed a dark chamber.

"This must be it," Mr. Dalton said and tried to push his way through.

"Stay back, Dalton," Mr. Lowell barred his way.

"I wouldn't do that, if I were you," Mr. Dalton said. "I'm armed."

"And so am I," replied Mr. Lowell nonchalantly.

Of course he is! Uncle Albert and I moved closer together. Were we about to witness a gangster-style shootout in an ancient Egyptian temple?

"There's no need for that," James said and moved between the two men. "Let's just see what we've got here, and then we'll decide how to deal with the situation."

"What we've got here," Mr. Dalton said smugly, "is the gateway to immense wealth and eternal health."

Perhaps momentarily awed by his words, no one stopped Mr. Dalton as he walked into the black chamber. He played the beam of his torch across the dark walls and floor. "What is this?!" he exclaimed.

We all stepped in to see better, and a cool dampness enveloped us. The chamber appeared to be a large sphere, its rounded walls roughly dug out of the naked earth.

"I don't understand!" Mr. Dalton exclaimed again, twisting around and staring at the empty walls in disbelief. "The treasure! Someone has taken the treasure!"

"So Mr. Hargrave died for nothing," I whispered. "Did you kill Mr. Hargrave?" I asked, glaring at Mr. Dalton, incensed. "Did you kill him so you could get access to this empty hole?!"

"What?! What are you on about, woman?" Mr. Dalton said, dragging his gaze from the wall to me.

"You've been after the treasure in this temple ever since you set foot on the boat and heard Mr. Hargrave speak of its existence. And when we discovered the temple, you killed him so you could keep the treasure for yourself. But someone beat you to it."

"Lady Caroline," Mr. Dalton said, adopting a condescending tone, "I've known about the alleged existence of this temple long before you even heard of it. I didn't need to murder anyone. My clients have enough money to buy anything. And anyone. All I had to do was wait for someone to find the temple and its treasure."

"What about your spy here?" I said, nodding towards the man with the scar. "Maybe he killed Mr. Hargrave."

"Ashraf here," he said nodding to the man with the scar, "is not exactly the type of man Mr. Hargrave's foreman would have let into the temple," Mr. Dalton answered. "No, if anyone killed Mr. Hargrave, it was one of the people from the boat. And who says he was killed, anyway?"

I was not about to reveal Mr. Lowell's theory about the wound on Mr. Hargrave's head.

Mr. Dalton examined my face for a while. "Isn't the killer usually the one who pretends to have found the body?" he said, smirking.

"Miss Kershaw is unlikely to have been the killer," I said, without elaborating on my reasoning.

"Why? Was she sweet on him?" he asked, quite crassly. "I saw how they looked at each other. Okay, how about that silly woman, Mrs. Gladstone? I saw her walking this way, as though looking for someone. Always going on and on about another death. Well, in the end, she got one more than she bargained for."

Mr. Dalton really was quite heartless.

"What would her reason be for killing Mr. Hargrave?" I said, wondering if he knew something.

"I don't know. I'm not a detective. Anyhow, I'm not interested in any of that. I did not kill anyone. Now I just have to find out who stole the treasure." He turned around to appraise the empty chamber. "Greedy scum. They didn't even leave one gold ingot."

As he said this, Uncle Albert began to chuckle. "You are wrong, Mr. Dalton, my boy," he said as he stepped further into the chamber and examined its walls with his torch. "No one has stolen the treasure. This is a treasure chamber, but of a very different kind. This is a chamber devoted to accommodating the god of eternal life—Khepri, the dung beetle. Rather large, but a beetle burrow nonetheless." He chuckled to himself in delight.

Mr. Dalton turned sharply around to look at the earthen chamber again. "It can't be." He barely breathed out the words.

"Lord Tatham is quite right," an accented voice said behind us.

We all turned around again, and this time we saw the fez maker's nephew. Next to him was the young Egyptian man from the museum. Their handguns were drawn out and pointed at us. Behind them were a few other people dressed in European suits and fezzes. A golden scarab pin glittered on the lapel of each man.

"You!" I said. "What are you doing here?! What is going on?" I was utterly confused.

"Forgive me, Lady Caroline," the fez-maker's nephew said, "for our little game. Sending the fez to your uncle was the only way to safeguard the code. I knew Mr. Dalton and his assistant would be less likely to attack a European, especially a Lord. They had no reservations about ransacking my uncle's humble workshop."

I shook my head. "I still don't understand..."

"Let me explain myself better," the fez-maker's nephew said. "My uncle and I, and all these men,"—he indicated the men behind him—"are members of the ancient cult of Khepri. We believe in reincarnation and eternal life. The scarab is our symbol. Ever since ancient times, we have been an underground organization, safeguarding the knowledge of the beetle-god. We recognize each other by the golden pins on our suits." He touched the pin on his lapel, and his companions did the same, murmuring something.

"Our cult has always been secret—even the pharaohs feared it," he continued. "But it survived the pharaohs, the Greeks, the Ottomans, and then the French and the British. Our members were persecuted and oppressed over the millennia, and were forced to practice their beliefs in the shadows, like the scarab beetle. And with time, the location of our temple was lost and forgotten. The only thing we had left was the pattern of scarabs you see embroidered on the lining of your uncle's fez. The pattern was passed down from father to son, from uncle to nephew, making its way down the millennia.

"The legend passed down along with it spoke of a lost temple containing great riches and the secret to eternal life. The pattern of scarabs was the key to unlocking this secret. We thought that one day, the scarabs will lead us to the lost temple and its treasure.

"And then, when Lord Chatfield and his brother came to Cairo to let the authorities know that they'd discovered a reference to a temple of Khepri, we knew the time was near. And when my friend here,"—he nodded to the young man from the museum—"heard Mr. Hargrave speak to you at the museum, and invite you to the dig, we saw an opportunity to smuggle the scarab pattern to Luxor under Mr. Dalton's nose, as you say."

I heard Mr. Dalton scoff behind me.

"We have our own spies everywhere," the fez-maker's nephew continued his story, "and as news of this undiscovered temple spread, we learned that Mr. Dalton had been contacted by some collectors in Germany who were very interested in the secret to eternal life. They were prepared to pay anything for it. So Mr. Dalton set about getting his hands on the scarab pattern, and I set about hiding it from him."

The pieces quickly fell into place. "But his spy caught on to your plan," I said, glancing at the man with the scar, standing in the shadows. "And you, Mr. Dalton," I said, turning now to him, "made sure to be on the same boat as my uncle. Did you rifle through my uncle's room?"

The American only smirked. "Where was that cloth hidden? I was sure it was in the fez," he said, nodding towards the silk in my uncle's hands. "Not that it matters now..."

"Inside the carpet," I answered. "The large one."

Mr. Dalton nodded, then he turned to the fez-maker's nephew. "So, you think there is no chance of any real treasure?"

"I believe we have misinterpreted the legend. Our forefathers believed that dung beetles were immortal. They were the symbol of rebirth and eternal life. And what treasure is greater than immortality? It's only fitting that a temple devoted to Khepri would have a chamber devoted to beetles. It is the most divine of creatures on earth, after all." All the men touched their golden pins again.

Uncle Albert nodded in agreement and beamed.

CHAPTER 27

We made our way back to the hotel. The temple's guards were paid off by Mr. Lowell to keep quiet. And since we were not taking anything out of the temple, they didn't haggle much over the price.

Ahead of us were the members of the cult of Khepri. Mr. Dalton was walking alongside them, busily trying to negotiate the sale of some of the cult's antiques. Resigned to the bitter fact that there was no prospect of treasure, he was nevertheless loath to lose out on the opportunity to sell something related to the cult to his German clients.

Uncle Albert walked slowly by my side, leaning heavily on my arm. He was murmuring sweet nothings into the night's air, recounting everything that had happened since we'd descended into the temple. I doubted there was anyone in our little procession more satisfied with the culmination of events than Uncle Albert. Even the members of the cult had to be a little disappointed—though they hid it quite admirably —that the secret they had been harboring for millennia was just a giant beetle dugout. But to Uncle Albert, it was pure divine poetry.

James was walking next to me on my other side. I could feel the warmth radiating from his body, and it gave me security.

My mind lingered on our understanding. Why was I so hesitant to let him make a formal proposal and a proper announcement? Did I not want to be his wife? No, that was not it. Not really. What I truly wanted was to be near him. To be his confidant, his friend, his companion. I knew that one day we would be married. But I didn't know how soon that would be. While I wanted to spend the rest of my life with James, I was not certain I wanted to assume the responsibilities of being his wife quite yet. At least, I did not want to do all the things wives were supposed to do— run a household, think of ways to advance one's husband's political or business career, and invite the right people to dinner. How burdensome! What I wanted was to travel and just be with him. And experience things. Just like we were doing now, but perhaps not in the company of the Royal Society.

I knew I had to speak to him about it. And I was certain he would understand how important this freedom I was experiencing now was to me. But would he settle for an unconventional life? And what about children? Of course, I wanted children. But they did tie one down to one place...

Perhaps this was a topic better discussed with James. And yet, I worried that if I shared my deepest fears with him, I would lose him...*Enough,* I told myself. James was not such a man! Fatigue was filling my head with melancholy thoughts.

I searched for another topic to occupy my mind and latched on to Mr. Hargrave's death again.

If Mr. Dalton was not the killer, then who was? And could one trust Mr. Dalton's word? And was Mr. Hargrave even murdered, or was it just a terrible accident? The red mark on Mr. Hargrave's neck, that had made the local police suspect foul play, had been explained away. The only thing that suggested murder was Mr. Lowell's conjecture that the gash on Mr. Hargrave's head was not made by a falling rock, but by someone hitting him on the head from a much closer distance.

Was Mr. Lowell's theory accurate? He had only seen the wound for a few moments. He was not a doctor. He had not examined the body.

How could Mr. Lowell be certain?

If Mr. Dalton was eliminated from the list of suspects, who did that leave? Only Mr. Kershaw, Mrs. Gladstone, Miss Parker and Mrs. Babcock.

Mr. Kershaw was a likely suspect. He had not liked Mr. Hargrave, and had wanted the dig's concession for himself. Had he murder for it? If he had, why now? He'd been in Egypt all this time, and he'd had plenty of opportunities, arguably, to take his revenge on the two brothers. So why murder Mr. Hargrave now? Was it the discovery of the temple that had made him crack?

Or had it been something else? Had Mr. Kershaw discovered his daughter's engagement to Mr. Hargrave? Had he killed him because he hated the man so much he did not want him for a son-in-law? But that was rather extreme. And yet, why had Miss Kershaw been so worried that her father would find out about her engagement? What had she been afraid of?

I cast my mind back to all the evidence I had about the murder. Mr. Kershaw had plenty of motives. Did he have the opportunity? Yes, I concluded.

Mrs. Gladstone's ramblings about a curse and the prediction of a death to come might have given him the idea to get rid of Mr. Hargrave. With Lord Chatfield out of the way, eliminating Mr. Hargrave would open up the possibility of securing the dig concession. Plus, Mr. Kershaw had more than the necessary knowledge to set up the mummy at the camp and write the message. And he did not have an alibi for the time of Mr. Hargrave's death.

Neither did Mrs. Gladstone or Mrs. Babcock, I conceded. Why had Mrs. Babcock been so quick to give Mrs. Gladstone an alibi? Was it because she didn't have one herself? But what could her reason for killing Mr. Hargrave be?

And what could Mrs. Gladstone's reason be, for that matter?

I sighed. I was missing a crucial piece of the puzzle, something that would help all of these scattered observations make sense.

Was the crucial piece something to do with Mrs. Gladstone's identity? Why had Mr. Hargrave attempted to confirm her identity with the authorities? And why had he confronted her about it on the boat? Was that enough of a reason to have Mrs. Gladstone kill him?

But what about the mummy? Would Mrs. Gladstone know where to find the mummy and how to write that message? She pretended not to know anything about Egyptology. But she also pretended to be a novice medium, and I was certain that was not true.

And what about Miss Parker? I knew so little about her. Had I misinterpreted her glances towards Mr. Hargrave? Were the glances I'd taken for amorous been filled with hatred instead? Had she met him while he'd visited New York? But what could he have done to her to have her hate him enough to kill him? Was it a broken engagement? Unrequited love?

My mind jumped to Alistair's conversation with Miss Parker in the Cook and Son office. What if Miss Parker discovered what boat Mr. Hargrave was on and that's why she ended up buying tickets for our boat? I needed to learn more about Miss Parker.

And that left only Mrs. Babcock. What would

Mrs. Babcock's motive be? She'd lost everything. Her employer, her employment. Was anyone likely to hire a female secretary in Egypt? Would she ever get to work on another dig again?

As I walked, I stared at Mr. Lowell's back. Was Mrs. Babcock truly my last suspect? What about Mr. Lowell? What did I really know about him?

I considered the question for a few moments. What was he really doing in Egypt? According to James, Mr. Lowell had expectations from some distant uncle who had paid his school fees. Was that uncle the old Lord Chatfield, the one who had died ten years ago? What if Mr. Lowell never received his expectation and had come to take his revenge? Admittedly, it was a stretch, but the way Mr. Lowell popped up on our boat as we arrived in Luxor was rather suspicious. And then he popped up again right after Mr. Hargrave's death. Had he been down in the passageways of the temple, waiting in the darkness, biding his time to kill Mr. Hargrave? But why?

What if Mr. Lowell had also been after the treasure? I pondered the look I'd seen on his face when the secret door had receded. Had it been greed or just pure fascination?

I sighed again. Nothing really made much sense. I was left with suspects that didn't really have strong motives.

Leaning on James' shoulder, I let the night's cool air wash over me.

Suddenly, an uncomfortable thought pricked me. Was I to blame for Mr. Hargrave's death?

I lifted my head and stared out into the darkness of the night. It was I who'd brought up the legend, curse, and treasure that fateful evening when Lord Chatfield drowned. Had my curiosity set in motion these deadly events? If I had not asked about the legend, would Lord Chatfield still be alive? Would Mr. Hargrave?

Surely not! I could not be held responsible for other people's choices. And even if Mr. Hargrave's death turned out to be murder, the killer must have had a plan in mind long before I ever brought up the question of the treasure.

Deep in my soul, however, I was not quite convinced of my innocence in this matter. Did I bear moral responsibility for these deaths? I walked on with a heavy heart and a troubled mind.

CHAPTER 28

The next morning, I went to Uncle Albert's suite to check up on him. Last I had seen him the previous night, he'd been chatting away in the hotel lobby with the men from the Khepri cult.

Lightly knocking, I went in before Wilford had opened the door. I found the valet sitting at a desk by the window, with his back to me. Upon hearing me come in, he got up abruptly.

"Don't let me disturb you, Wilford," I said. "Please go back to your task. Is Uncle Albert here?" I looked about the room, but the old relation was conspicuously absent.

"His Lordship is in the gardens. News reached him that holes have started appearing in the Royal Society's nets stationed around the grounds. Lord Tatham suspects that some of the more unsavory members of the Society are sabotaging other members' nightly catch. He departed post-haste after receiving the distressing communication."

"It's more likely to be one of the hotel guests," I said.

"Quite so, My Lady," Wilford agreed, and

returned to his task at the desk.

I was quite at a loss as to what to do next. I lingered in Uncle's sitting room and looked at the titles of the books scattered about —all beetle related, unfortunately. I considered going into the gardens, but had no particular desire to get entangled in Royal Society business at the moment. I walked to the window and spied Poppy's sailboat. One felt awkward visiting one's friends impromptu when they were on their honeymoon. Withdrawing my gaze from the window, it happened to fall upon Wilford at the table.

"What are you doing, Wilford?!" I exclaimed. He was holding an aspirator in one hand and a brush in the other. But it was the state of the desk he was sitting at that had caught my attention. It was covered in newspapers, upon which sat numerous stone scarabs.

"I am in the process of cleaning and cataloging Lord Tatham's scarabs, My Lady," he answered.

"Where did he get all of these? There must be at least a score of them, if not more!"

"His Lordship rescued these twenty-seven stone scarabs from the collection, so to speak, of the late Lord Chatfield, on the day we boarded the boat up the Nile."

"I say! The crafty devil. Do you think Uncle will win?" I asked, referring to the Society's beetle and scarab competition. Uncle Albert had been quite sly to pilfer Lord Chatfield's golfing stash.

"Hard to say, My Lady. I hear Lord Packenham has been paying off a man at the Egyptian Museum in Cairo to supply him with fresh batches as they arrive at the institution from various digs. If rumors are true, Lord Packenham is up to thirty-two scarabs."

"There are so many of these about," I said, picking up a green-colored scarab from the desk and running it through my fingers. "I wonder how many of them are truly genuine. I wouldn't be surprised if there is a workshop somewhere producing them for the tourists. I say!" I cried as I discerned exactly what lay beneath the scarabs.

"Yes, My Lady?"

"The newspaper!" I pointed to the desk.

"My Lady?"

"May I see this newspaper? I recognize the headline. Is this the London edition from the day before we boarded the boat?"

"I believe you are correct, My Lady," Wilford said, peering at the date on the front of the newspaper. "Your uncle found it discarded on the boat and used it to collect the scarabs Lord Chatfield had left on the deck."

"May I see it?"

I watched with growing impatience as Wilford fetched a starched handkerchief, placed it on a side table, transferred all the scarabs, two by two, on the side table, dusted the pages of the paper, and folded them neatly back together before handing it to me. It took all my power of self-control not to snatch the paper from him.

"Of course!" I said, after perusing the article about the curse of the tomb of Ahmose and the death of Lord Chatfield's uncle in England. I'd read it once before, but had not paid much attention to it. "How silly of me! How did I not consider this as a motive before? Excuse me, Wilford. I need to find Mr. Lowell and then Poppy."

I abandoned the confused valet and headed for the hotel lobby.

"Mr. Lowell," I said into the telephone apparatus, "Lady Caroline here."

"Yes, Lady Caroline," he said from the other end. "What can I do for you?"

"Is it possible to check if any of the passengers from our Cook and Son boat were in England around the time Lord Chatfield's uncle died?"

"What do you have in mind?" Mr. Lowell asked.

"It's just a theory at the moment. I still need to collect a few more pieces of information. But I'll be curious to know what you can find out for me."

I headed to Poppy's dahabiya next. Thankfully, the mistress of the sailboat was having breakfast on its deck, so I didn't feel so bad about barging in uninvited.

"Oh, hello, Gassy!" She waved to me enthusiastically. "Come to tell us about your midnight adventure, have you? Apparently, it's the talk of the dahabiya crews up and down the river."

So much for Mr. Lowell paying off the guards. I climbed on board without commenting and filled her in on the details of the giant beetle hole while she finished up her fried eggs. Leopold was sitting under the thick shade of a sun umbrella, straw hat on, eating something that looked suspiciously like porridge with minced dates.

"It's good for his digestion," Poppy said, following my glance. "So, if that American chap is not the killer, then who is left?"

"I would not write him off quite yet," I said. "I've had a revelation this morning. I'd been thinking about this whole thing the wrong way."

"How do you mean?"

"Until now, I believed that the dig site and its temple were why Mr. Hargrave was killed."

"If he was killed," Poppy objected, sticking to her curse thesis.

I inclined my head in acquiescence. "But there is another reason someone might have wanted him dead," I said.

"And what's that?"

"Inheritance!" I said triumphantly. "So the question now is, who inherits?"

"Inherits what exactly?" Poppy said, not quite following me.

"The title of Earl of Chatfield and all that comes with it—land, property, income, status, whatnot."

"Ah, the peerage," Poppy said. "Then it would have to be a man. At least that's what Leopold tells me about primogeniture." She smiled at her husband and he beamed back at her.

I nodded. "Yes, primogeniture, succession through the firstborn son. Tell me, what happens if the firstborn son dies?" I said.

"The peerage goes to his younger brother," Leopold spoke up for the first time. As the firstborn son in his family and the heir apparent, he was well versed in these things.

"And if this younger brother also dies?" I asked for Poppy's benefit, though I knew the answer.

"The title goes to the next younger brother, and if there are no brothers left, then to an uncle," Leopold said, his tone slightly bewildered, as if to say that as the daughter of an Earl, I should know quite well how titles progressed through the family tree.

"And if he's dead?" I asked. I could see Poppy's eyes lighting up, while Leopold's countenance was becoming dimmer. She had caught on to my theory. He probably thought I should be excommunicated from the upper class.

"You mean, with Lord Chatfield, his brother, and their uncle dead, the title will now go to another male relative," Poppy said.

"That's right. The title of the Earl of Chatfield now goes to a collateral branch. Some distant male descendent through the male line. A cousin.

The British newspapers were kind enough to tell us that a Mr. Hargrave attended the funeral of the uncle in question in England." I waved the newspaper in my hand. "But we know that it was not our Mr. Hargrave who attended. He was here, in Egypt, at the time."

"So there is another Mr. Hargrave?" Poppy asked. "One of the men from the boat?"

"Most likely," I said, a wisp of a thought forming in my mind.

"But who?" Poppy pressed.

"That's what I'm here to find out," I said. "I need to look at your *Debrett's Peerage* volume."

Poppy fetched the thick red tome, and we had no difficulty locating the entry for *Chatfield, Earl of*. What proved to be rather more difficult was to wrestle out of the dense text which member of which collateral branch would inherit next. There were so many descendants of 3rd sons of the 2nd Earl, and 2nd sons of the 4th Earl, and so on, with so many dates of births and deaths and marriages thrown in, that I was soon feeling lightheaded.

"Oh, it's no good," I lamented and closed the volume.

"What now?" Poppy asked.

"We ask the experts!" I said and set off back to the lobby.

My aunts, Mable, Mavis and Myrtle, preoccupied as they were with spiritual matters and the beyond, were also quite astute in matters of primogeniture and peerage. After all, among our class, death was closely linked to inheritance. It was rumored that more than one contentious estate had consulted dear aunt Myrtle on matters of rightful heirs. I sent off a cable to England having full faith in my aunts' abilities to find who the title went to next, even before the authorities did.

"Ah, Lady Caroline," the hotel's concierge said. "While you were out, a message came through for you from Mr. Lowell. He is requesting that you telephone him at his office."

"Hello, Lady Caroline," he said from the other end of the line after we were connected. "I have some news that you might find interesting. First, no one from your boat party was in England at the time of Lord Chatfield's uncle's death. All were either here already, or on a boat traveling to Egypt. Second, the local authorities are now quite certain that the death of Mr. Hargrave was not an accident. They will be coming round shortly to interview you all again. I'm sorry to say that our little excursion to the temple last night might not look good. But fret not, I have been speaking to the British High Commissioner who will smooth things over."

"Thank you," I said into the telephone. One didn't want to get on the wrong side of the Egyptian authorities.

"But there is another piece of news, this

one pertaining to Mrs. Gladstone. We've been monitoring her, as you suggested, and instead of boarding the earliest available boat to New York, which was yesterday, she purchased tickets for a boat to Italy. I'm not entirely positive how you knew she would not get on the New York boat, but well done."

"Uhm..." I said. That Mrs. Gladstone was about to travel to Italy was a complete surprise to me. I had not expected it.

"Anyhow, the Egyptian authorities are bringing her to Luxor for interviews as we speak. I will see you at the hotel tomorrow." And with that, he rang off.

The news about Mrs. Gladstone perplexed me. I had no explanation for it. The only reason I had suggested the authorities should watch her was because she was rather suspicious.

I stood at reception for a few minutes, trying to collect my thoughts. Mr. Hargrave was murdered. Who was to inherit the Earl of Chatfield peerage? And was Mrs. Gladstone trying to flee from the authorities by going to Italy?

My eyes landed on a gentleman sitting in one of the deep armchairs in the lobby, reading an American newspaper. I moved closer to get a better look. There, on the front page, was a sensational headline about The Curse of the Scarab. I inched towards him, squinting to make out the rest.

The man lowered his newspaper. "Can I help

you, miss?"

I blushed. "I say, would you mind terribly if I borrowed your paper? After you are done with it, of course!"

He looked at me quizzically. "Be my guest." He handed the newspaper to me. "It's all this boloney about a curse."

As I had perceived, the article was about the death of Mr. Gladstone. A hapless servant, who the neighbors had seen going into the Gladstone residence at night, had been arrested for Mr. Gladstone's murder.

The value of the article, however, revealed itself on the interior pages, where a rather grainy picture of Mrs. Gladstone, with the note that she was currently on an Egyptian cruise, was attached. It looked like a passport photo, taken when she had been somewhat younger. I stared at the photograph. There definitely was a resemblance, I conceded.

Then I noticed it.

Mr. Hargrave had been correct. Unless the Mrs. Gladstone we'd met on the boat had undergone some ancient Egyptian miracle procedure, the woman we knew as Mrs. Gladstone was not the person in the newspaper.

"So that's how they did it," I said to myself after some time, and took the newspaper with me.

CHAPTER 29

I had spent the rest of the previous day cabling messages back and forth with my aunts in England. It was the fifth and final telegram, which had arrived this morning, that had supplied me with the ultimate piece of the puzzle. I knew who had murdered Mr. Hargrave, and I knew why.

We were gathered in one of the hotel's smaller lounge rooms overlooking the garden, furnished with comfortable sofas and armchairs. Present were Mrs. Babcock, Mr. Dalton, and Mr. and Miss Kershaw, who were all here on my invitation. Not in attendance were the members of the Royal Society, who I was quite certain had no involvement in the death of Mr. Hargrave. The members of the Society could be seen from the room's windows, tottering about the garden with sweep nets in a desperate bid to boost their beetle numbers before the final count.

James had somehow wriggled out of his duties and was sitting in a corner. I smiled at him. He winked back.

I had explained enough of my theory to Mr. Lowell to have him keep the Egyptian authorities at bay for the moment. It was on account of his urging that the police had allowed me to proceed with my little assembly. But I had not revealed to Mr. Lowell who I suspected to be the killer. He was standing near James, observing me with tense interest.

Two Egyptian policemen were standing on the other side of the room by the door. They lent the gathering the appropriate level of legitimacy. And it was their presence that had guaranteed everyone's attendance. The two men wore a bemused expression as they observed the people in the room.

Standing near the policemen, but separate from everyone else, was a man I didn't recognize. He had the supercilious look of a petty official, so he was not the British High Commissioner, as I'd presumed at first glance.

The door opened abruptly, and in walked Mrs. Gladstone and Miss Parker. Behind them was another Egyptian policeman. I smiled. Their presence would make the reveal more effectual.

The two women looked careworn and took the two empty chairs that had been left for them without making eye contact with the rest of the attendees. Miss Parker was ashen-faced and her eyes were wide with trepidation. I examined Mrs. Gladstone's face. There was no sign of a cosmetic procedure. Yes, I was positive. This was someone else entirely.

A whisper of surprise had passed through the room upon the entrance of the two women, but no one had greeted them. Mr. Dalton smirked, Mr. Kershaw frowned. Mrs. Babcock lifted an eyebrow, and Miss Kershaw stared at them with an empty gaze.

It was time to begin.

I was sitting in a chair, facing my audience, with all my newspapers and telegrams laid out on a low table in front of me. My puzzle pieces. All I had to do now was put them together in order. Mr. Dalton was peering at them, trying to make them out.

"Thank you all for coming," I began. "As you probably know, the Egyptian police have determined that Mr. Hargrave's death was murder, based on the type of wound he sustained." I wondered if Mr. Lowell had played a part in that verdict. "And they suspect that one of the people in this room killed him."

People shifted in their seats, but no one contradicted me. I cast a quick glance at Miss Kershaw. She was staring at the ground at her feet.

"The police have been kind enough to humor me and allow me to gather you all here," I continued. "I believe I know who killed Mr. Hargrave and why."

Mr. Dalton scoffed. Mr. Kershaw reached for his daughter's hand and squeezed it. I wondered if she'd told him about her attachment to Mr.

Hargrave. The three other women—Mrs. Babcock, Mrs. Gladstone and Miss Parker—gasped.

I ignored Mr. Dalton's derision and pressed on. "I am certain that Mr. Hargrave was killed because he was the heir to the Earl of Chatfield title. With Mr. Hargrave dead, the title now passes on to a distant relative—another Hargrave from a remote family branch." I paused and looked around. "And here today, among us, sits a Hargrave."

The statement brought out a few more gasps. The more perceptive among the group looked from Mr. Dalton to Mr. Kershaw. Mr. Dalton glared menacingly at everyone, while Mr. Kershaw looked around him in a more subdued manner.

I stole a glance at Mr. Lowell and examined his face. I wondered if my revelation had surprised him. I wondered if he knew which Hargrave relative I was talking about. But he looked back at me with an unwavering gaze.

"It's not me," Mr. Dalton said and laughed, though he shifted uncomfortably and flashed his eyes towards the Egyptian policemen by the door.

Mr. Kershaw turned to his daughter as though looking for confirmation that he was not the heir, either. She shook her head and smiled at him.

I looked down at the papers in front of me. "But I'm getting ahead of myself," I said. "In order to understand why Mr. Hargrave was murdered, we have to go back to the beginning. It all started with the death of an old man, the brothers' uncle in England. A death brought on, the newspapers proclaimed, by an ancient curse."

"Don't tell us that the uncle was also murdered," Mr. Dalton said, having regained some of his confidence.

"I've considered that. The uncle's funeral was attended by a Mr. Hargrave and I wondered if that was our killer. It was certainly possible for someone to murder the old uncle and then make it to Egypt on time for the murder of Mr. Hargrave in the temple. After all, the British newspapers are sent to Egypt on the boats which bring the tourists. If the newspaper announcing the uncle's death had already arrived from England—I read about the death and curse in the British press the day before we boarded our steamer up the Nile—so could've the killer.

"But there is no indication that the uncle was murdered. And all of us were already either in Egypt, or traveling to Egypt, at the time of his death. Plus, at the time, no one had any interest in killing the old man in England. The killer's plan began to form later. But the death of the uncle is the first clue in our mystery. What we need to understand, in order to follow the killer's logic, is that the uncle had been second in line for the Earl of Chatfield title."

I took a sip of water to gather my thoughts. "As we sailed up the Nile, Lord Chatfield died. There is no question his death was an accident. And then

Mrs. Gladstone held her seance and proclaimed another death."

Upon hearing her name, Mrs. Gladstone looked up. Her gaze appraised me as though wondering where I would lead to next.

"I'm convinced that the murderer did not set off with the purpose of killing. But as events unfolded, the killer began to see these events as predestined, as fate. With the uncle and Lord Chatfield dead, the only one who stood between the Earldom and this distant heir was our Mr. Hargrave."

"Wait a minute," Mr. Dalton objected. "How did Mrs. Gladstone know that Mr. Hargrave was going to die? Only the killer would know that." He turned and scowled at her. "Arrest her and let's get it over with."

"You forget, Mr. Dalton," I said, "that Mrs. Gladstone is unlikely to inherit the peerage. She is a woman. Mrs. Gladstone, I think, had her own reasons for predicting death. But those are not of importance at the moment. You are right, however, her predictions played right into the killer's hands.

"From the beginning, this case has been muddled by the specter of the deadly curse. We were all fascinated by the possibility that all these deaths had supernatural causes. And that was what the killer hoped we'd assume as well.

"But if we dismiss supernatural causes, then we notice that two events occurred in close succession that could have led to Mr. Hargrave's murder—his brother's death on the river, and the discovery of the Temple of Khepri. Following each of these threads leads to a different group of suspects.

"In my investigation,"—Mr. Dalton let out a derisive chuckle—"I chose to follow the thread connected to the discovery of the temple first. After all, Mr. Hargrave's murder occurred inside the temple, immediately after the temple's discovery. And that thread led me to Mr. Kershaw and Mr. Dalton as suspects. Mr. Kershaw because he blamed the brothers for losing the dig site, and Mr. Dalton because he was after the treasure hidden inside the temple."

"We've been over this before," Mr. Dalton protested. "And it's not me."

"I also have to object to your reasoning," Mr. Kershaw spoke up. "Why would I kill anyone over a dig site?"

"Because with the discovery of the temple, the site had become that much more valuable. Perhaps you hoped to win the site concession next," I suggested.

"Fat chance of that happening," Mr. Kershaw said. "Bunch of fools running the Department of Antiquities." He crossed his arms and stared into space, brooding.

"Daddy got news today that he is unlikely to be given the concession," Miss Kershaw added.

I smiled sympathetically. Politics always seemed to get in the way of doing the right thing and giving the job to the most capable man.

"However," I went back to my train of thought, "it wasn't until I chanced again upon the article I had read in Cairo, about the death of the uncle in England, that I realized my mistake. I had failed to follow a second possibility—that it was Lord Chatfield's death that had led directly to Mr. Hargrave's murder. I had failed to consider that there were other Hargrave males in line for the peerage. Mr. Hargrave's death was about inheritance.

"The deaths in the Hargrave family had nothing to do with curses, ancient tombs and secret temples. But Mr. Hargrave's killer wanted us to think that they did, because if the deaths of the uncle and Lord Chatfield could be written off as accidents, or explained away by a deadly curse, then so could Mr. Hargrave's death.

"Remember the mummy at the camp? The killer set up the mummy to remind us of the curse. The killer wanted the curse to be fresh in our minds because Mr. Hargrave's murder was coming. Perhaps the killer had not decided how or when, but nevertheless, Mr. Hargrave's fate was sealed."

"So then it had to be Mrs. Gladstone," Mr. Dalton said again. "She is the only one who predicted a death."

"Yes, but Mrs. Gladstone knows nothing about

mummies or hieroglyphs. No, I was convinced, even then, that the mummy prank was carried out by an Egyptologist."

The archeologists looked at each other as though trying to decide which one of them was the killer.

"But wait a minute," Mr. Dalton objected. "How did the killer know to be on our boat? You said the killer did not set off to kill Mr. Hargrave. So why was the killer on the boat at all?"

"Was the killer on our boat?" I asked. "The mummy accident and the murder of Mr. Hargrave happened after we'd arrived in Luxor. But I'd wrestled with that question as well," I admitted. I looked around the room at all the men present. It was time to make my revelation. "I now know that the killer happened to be on the boat by chance, or rather, we happened to be on the same boat as the killer by chance. But as events unfolded—the death of Lord Chatfield and the prediction of more deaths to come—she began to view her presence on the boat as divine intervention."

"She?!" Miss Kershaw exclaimed. "I think you mean *he*."

I shook my head. "The murderer is a woman," I said.

CHAPTER 30

"I'm confused," Mr. Dalton said. "If the killer is a woman, why would she kill Mr. Hargrave for his title?"

"Because the title goes to her son," I said.

Mr. Kershaw flashed a shy glance at his daughter. Only the slight flutter of her curls told me she'd shaken her head. So he knew of their engagement. But even if Miss Kershaw was with child, and the child was a boy, an illegitimate child could not inherit his father's title.

"But you said a Hargrave was among us," Mr. Dalton countered.

I nodded. "Yes, because the woman in question was married to a Hargrave. A John Hargrave. A distant cousin of Lord Chatfield's. After her husband's death, I believe Mrs. John Hargrave was so ashamed of having to work for a living, that she chose to use a different name for work." I saw several people glance at Miss Parker curiously. I think they were noticing her properly for the first time. "But she didn't use her maiden name, as is sometimes customary," I continued. "You see, she is listed under her maiden name in *Debrett's Peerage*, as married to John Hargrave of the collateral branch descended from the second son of the 5th Earl of Chatfield. I believe she was so embarrassed to be registered in a peerage volume and yet have to work, that she chose to use her mother's maiden name instead. I had to leave it up to some very clever old ladies in England to dig that fact up. Isn't that right Mrs. Babcock?"

She looked up, shocked. "Me!" She laughed. "You are completely wrong."

"No, I checked," I said. "Your son, William Hargrave, is the heir to the title. I have confirmation from London." I picked up one of the telegrams from the table. "But this telegram is only the definitive proof that your son inherits. You had told me yourself that after your husband's death, the Hargraves gave you a job and paid your son's school fees. Why would they do that? Because you are a Hargrave by marriage."

She glared at me. "Yes, instead of fulfilling their familial obligations and providing for me, they offered me a job. And it was Lord Chatfield who suggested I use a different name. Didn't want to appear nepotistic, he said." She scoffed. "But I didn't kill Mr. Hargrave. His death was an accident, whatever the Egyptian *experts* might say."

"No, the police are quite certain that it was murder. Something to do with the wound," I said, feigning ignorance in order to spare Miss Kershaw the details.

"But you have no proof," Mrs. Babcock said. "Anyone could have killed him. I have an alibi. I walked into that chamber together with Mrs. Gladstone to find Mr. Hargrave already dead."

"Yes, Mrs. Gladstone provided you with the perfect alibi. She probably assumed that you were providing her with an alibi, but it was actually the other way round. It was you who needed a witness to account for your movements."

Mrs. Babcock's eyes darted around, her face growing red. "Why don't you ask Miss Kershaw what she was doing with the body," she said angrily. "I saw her tear something away from Mr. Hargrave's neck. Maybe she killed him for it."

And that's when I knew Mrs. Babcock had trapped herself.

The Egyptian policemen stirred upon hearing about the amulet. I looked at Mr. Lowell and shook my head. He bounded over to the Egyptians and said something to them that made them stand down.

"How could you have seen Miss Kershaw?" I asked Mrs. Babcock. "If the first time you set foot in that chamber, as you claim, was when you walked in with Mrs. Gladstone, you could not have seen Miss Kershaw take the amulet. Miss Kershaw is positive the amulet was already in her pocket by the time you came in."

"So she admits it!" Mrs. Babcock cried out.

I ignored her. "The only way you could have seen Miss Kershaw take the amulet was if you had been in the chamber already when Miss Kershaw found Mr. Hargrave's body. You killed Mr. Hargrave, saw Miss Kershaw find him and take the amulet, then used one of the many dark corridors to make it appear as though you had just walked in. Meeting Mrs. Gladstone was a lucky coincidence."

Mrs. Babcock remained silent.

"Your other mistake," I continued, "was the mummy." Mrs. Babcock looked at me sharply, something akin to uncertainty flashing across her eyes. "Who could get around the camp unnoticed by the guards? Who could go into Lord Chatfield's tent and the tent containing the mummy without arousing suspicion? Someone who the guards knew well. To them, you were neither a stranger nor suspicious. They didn't pay attention to you going in and out of tents, setting up your charade. Or rather, I should say, they would not have paid any attention to you, had they not been sleeping on the job.

"And tell me, why did you feel the need to inform me that you could not read hieroglyphics? Was it so I would not suspect that you had written the message pinned to the mummy?"

"You have absolutely no proof," she said and laughed.

"I think we have enough," I said and glanced at

Mr. Lowell. He nodded and motioned to the two Egyptian policemen. They walked Mrs. Babcock out of the room. Mr. Lowell followed behind them.

As I watched them leave, I mused that the murder of Mr. Hargrave had been about treasure after all. Not one hidden in an Egyptian temple. It was the treasure of power and privilege that came with the title of the Earl of Chatfield.

"So it was Mrs. Babcock?" Mr. Dalton said.

I nodded.

"And no one knew about her being related to the Hargraves?" he asked. "Or that her son was in line to inherit?"

"Lord Chatfield and Mr. Hargrave knew, of course. But there was no reason for them to worry that Mrs. Babcock, or Mrs. Hargrave, I should say, would murder them. Her son was fairly back in the line. And I think the maiden name arrangement suited her. Imagine the mortification she would have felt if one of her son's friends discovered that his mother was working in Egypt," I said, certain that I had grasped some of Mrs. Babcock's motivation.

"So there is no question that her son will inherit?" Mr. Dalton asked.

"No question. His right of succession is not diminished by his mother's crime," I said. "And I am certain she was well aware of that. But she probably did it for herself as well. If her scheme had succeeded, and Mr. Hargrave's death was ruled an accident, she would have been free of a job she hated and a country she loathed." I thought back to all the times Mrs. Babcock had condemned Egypt and the Egyptians.

"I knew Mrs. Babcock was the evil presence on the boat," Mrs. Gladstone spoke up for the first time. She looked quite relaxed now that Mrs. Babcock had been led away and someone else was arrested for the murder of Mr. Hargrave. "Time for us to go, Daisy." She got up from her chair and made to leave. "I don't know why they brought us all the way back to Luxor on the train for this."

"Actually, Mrs. Gladstone," I said, turning my attention now to her little scheme. "I wonder, why did you choose to travel to Italy, rather than return to New York?"

"Why not?" She raised her chin at me. "Mr. Gladstone's already dead. Nothing I can do about it. The funeral has come and gone. When am I going to go to Europe again?"

I smiled. That was probably a very candid statement. I pulled the American newspaper from my pile of papers. "Tell me, what happened to your rather prominent mole, right here on the left cheek? Even in this grainy photograph, it's quite visible." I pointed to the newspaper.

Mrs. Gladstone went pale and sat back down with a thud. Miss Parker sat down as well, looking just as pale.

The question had caught the attention of Mr.

Dalton, who turned to stare at Mrs. Gladstone's face.

"Is that what Mr. Hargrave had noticed? Is that why he confronted you on the boat?" I asked.

Mrs. Gladstone barely nodded.

"I told her to wear it," Miss Parker spoke up, "but she wouldn't listen. She had a fake mole to wear, but she was too lazy to put it on every day. Said no one knows Mrs. Gladstone here. She applied it only when going through customs and places that check your travel documents. But she thought it made her so ugly. So she stopped wearing it in Egypt."

"That's why you were hiding her face from the journalists at the hotel," I said.

Miss Parker nodded.

"Plus, I was sweating under that thing," Mrs. Gladstone said. "The glue was always itching. I was going to scratch it off, and then what would we do? I was better off without it." She shook her head. "Until Mr. Hargrave noticed..."

"Who are you?" I said, although I had a theory.

"I'm Mrs. Parker and this is my daughter, Daisy Parker." The young woman smiled at me.

I pitied them. If my hunch was right, they were about to get in plenty of trouble with the law. The official-looking man by the wall made to move, but I gave him a look to say that there was more to come.

"You are a medium, from the Gas Something District of New York," I said.

"The Gas House District," Mrs. Parker said. "How did you know?" She squinted at me as though trying to determine if I were a medium as well.

I shrugged. "You came to Egypt in place of the real Mrs. Gladstone," I said. "The resemblance is quite uncanny between the two of you, except for the mole."

Mrs. Parker nodded. "And just my luck that out of all the boats in Egypt, we end up on the one with someone who has met Mrs. Gladstone. She visited the university to establish an interest in Egyptian culture, as she called it. Mr. Hargrave remembered her mole. I tried to laugh it off, but he didn't buy it."

"That was quite an unfortunate piece of bad luck, especially after Miss Parker chose a boat with no Americans on it."

"How did you know?" It was Miss Parker's turn to exclaim.

I shrugged again. "And there was more back luck to come—the deaths and the curse."

Mrs. Parker nodded.

"But why didn't you keep quiet? Why did you have to hold a seance?" I asked, incredulous. Why had she not kept out of the spotlight?

"I tried to warn her," Miss Parker said, "but she would not listen. It was Mr. Dalton that rubbed her the wrong way. Saying that mediums were not real. She wanted to show off."

"All of you were going to be so shocked when you found out that I predicted Mr. Gladstone's death," Mrs. Parker said, her voice laced with pride.

"But then Mr. Gladstone's death caught the attention of the world press. How did you ever think you were going to get away with it?" I asked.

"What did they try to get away with?" Mr. Dalton interrupted. "What have they done?"

"They helped Mrs. Gladstone, the real one, murder her husband," I said.

Miss Kershaw's blue eyes, which had grown pale during our discussion of Mr. Hargrave's death, now flashed with interest as she examined the two women with renewed curiosity.

"How did the idea come about?" I asked.

"Oh, it was all her idea, Mrs. Gladstone's," Mrs. Parker said. "She started coming for readings and she noticed that we looked alike. Except for the mole. Then she told me her husband is very rich, but a miser. So she came up with a plan. I travel to Egypt under her name and with her documents. Daisy comes with me as my companion. I've never traveled before. While I'm in Egypt, she has the perfect alibi. She stays behind, hides in another town, then goes back to New York and pushes her husband down the stairs. She knew her husband was going to get rid of the servants while she was on her travels. She gave him the idea, to save money."

"Why Egypt?" Miss Kershaw asked.

"It's so far away, no one was going to suspect her. Plus, no one she knew was planning a trip to Egypt."

"Where did she stay while she was supposed to be away?" I asked.

"She has a cabin in Upstate New York, where her mother lived as a girl. In the woods. She was to travel second class back to New York. She knew her husband's habits and the habits of their neighbors, so she was sure she could sneak into the house and no one would see her."

"But someone did see her, and they arrested an innocent servant," I countered.

"I'm sorry," Mrs. Parker said feebly.

The official now moved in. "Mrs. Parker, Miss Parker, I'm Mr. Johnson, a representative of the American Government in Egypt. I'd like you to accompany me."

CHAPTER 31

We were sitting in front of the fez-maker's shop in Cairo, sipping tea. It was ten days after the events in Luxor. The Royal Society had traveled down the Nile at a leisurely pace and stopped at all the sights along the way. We had arrived in Cairo the previous morning.

I was sitting next to James, our backs resting against the shop's wall. Gathered around the low table nearby, sitting on low stools, were Uncle Albert, the fez-maker, Mr. El Tarabishi, his nephew, Mr. Agib, and a plethora of store owners and sect of Khepri members. Uncle Albert, with the help of Mr. Agib's translation, was relating to his audience his adventure in the temple of Khepri. All gathered laughed heartily at the part about the secret dung beetle hole.

"You have to admit," James was saying, "Mrs. Gladstone's scheme was quite extraordinary. It was bound to fail."

"It could have worked," I countered. "Wife gone to Egypt, husband alone, falls down the stairs. Mrs. Gladstone is beyond all suspicion and inherits all that money. The scheme probably would have worked, if not for the Curse of the Scarab." I chuckled. "It probably would have worked if not for all these additional deaths, and the press getting a hold of Mr. Gladstone's death and lumping it in with the others. And it was in poor judgment for Mrs. Parker to do the seance. But she probably thought it was great fun."

"Why do you think Mrs. Parker was so quick to tell her story?" James said.

"There was no way to hide the charade any longer," I said."Not when the picture of the real Mrs. Gladstone was published. And I think she was tired of the whole thing. Keeping up this persona must have been exhausting."

A particularly rollicking laughter drew my attention back to the men's table. I gazed at the merriment playing on Uncle's face.

Uncle Albert had lost the beetle competition, but he didn't care. He had a glittering scarab pin adorning his lapel. The Khepri secret society had made him an honorary member. After all, he had discovered both their lost temple and the hidden chamber.

It was Alistair, or rather Lord Mantelbury, who had won the mummified trophy, but not before I had advised Poppy to part with some of Leopold's beetles. I thought the win would be good for Alistair's morale.

I had pointed out to Poppy that the Lords of the Royal Society would not look kindly upon an upstart surpassing them. They did not want the competition. And while the advice went against everything she believed about contests, she accepted it. I had assured her that Leopold would have no trouble getting accepted into the Royal Society. After all, ability had never been a prerequisite for joining. Membership was not predicated on how many beetles one had. It was based on what name one carried.

Watching my uncle talk animatedly about beetles, I thought back to a conversation I'd had with Mr. Agib. I had asked him why he had not contacted us again when we had reached Luxor. It had been safer for Uncle Albert that way, he'd said. Men from the cult were watching over him. Even on the boat.

I now heard Uncle Albert ask Mr. El Tarabishi if he was disappointed that the temple did not hold any treasure. The old man thought for a while then spoke slowly in Arabic. His nephew translated: "We've always been poor, and we'll remain poor. What one needs is to have something to eat, to be useful to his fellow men, and to have somewhere to sleep at night. Like the scarab beetle, we wake up each morning to do god's work another day."

Uncle Albert nodded and smiled beatifically, his golden pin glittering in the sun.

My thoughts wandered back to Mr. Hargrave's death. "I feel so sad for Miss Kershaw," I said. "I rather like her."

"Oh, I think I have some news on that front that might cheer you up," James said. "Ratty has used his connections in Egypt to secure the site for Mr. Kershaw. He is the best man for the job, anyway."

"That's rather nice of him," I said.

"I don't think it was an entirely altruistic act," James said. "He has rather taken a liking to Miss Kershaw."

"I hope Mr. Lowell and Miss Kershaw find happiness together."

"What about us?" James said and smiled. "Ready for a formal engagement?"

I smiled back at him, but I was not certain I was quite there yet.

"Speaking about engagements, did you read that Lady Morton is in Egypt, looking for a bride for Cecil?" I said, changing the subject.

The narrow lane rang out with James' laughter, and as I watched startled birds fly up into the blue sky, I knew all was well.

THE END

Thank you for reading *Secret of the Scarab*, Book 5 in the Lady Caroline Murder Mysteries series.

The adventures continue in Book 6.

One of my favorite parts about writing historical mysteries is the research. Visit https://

isabellabassett.com if you would like to read the **Historical Notes** for this book, or any of the other books in the Lady Caroline series.

On my website, you can also get in touch with me, sign up for my newsletter, learn more about this and other mystery series I write, or read about beautiful Switzerland, where I live.

MORE BOOKS BY ISABELLA BASSETT

The Old Bookstore Mysteries series about an old Swiss bookstore with a peculiar black cat.

Book 1: Out of Print

Book 2: Murderous Misprint

Book 3: Suspicious Small Print

Book 4: Reckless Reprint

Book 5: Incriminating Imprint

Book 6: Scandalous Snow Print

Book 7: Blackmail Blueprint

Made in the USA
Las Vegas, NV
01 December 2023